Delores Fossen

Lone Star Rescue

Hard Justice, Texas Series: Book 1

——— ☆ ———

By Delores Fossen
Copyright 2024 Delores Fossen
——— ☆ ———

For BJ Daniels and Julie Miller. So glad to be on this adventure with both of you.

Prologue
───── ☆ ─────

Major Rafe Cross focused on the mission. Get in and get out. Fast. A quick extraction. That was all he needed to think, see, feel, and hear right now.

Not the blinding, bleached white sand.

Or the blood that was on it.

Not the piercing shouts for help. The cries of pain. The smothering smoke from the burning buildings. Or the stench of ash and debris whipped up by the Pave Hawk chopper that was waiting on him and the rest of the team to do their jobs.

But, of course, Rafe couldn't shut out everything.

Especially that cold silence from his specific target.

She wasn't crying out for him to rescue her. Wasn't moaning. She wasn't doing or saying anything that the other survivors were. She was just lying there on the bloody sand where she'd fallen after a chunk of stone from one of those buildings had bashed into her while she'd been attempting to do her own extraction.

Another rescuer had moved in to get the kid that she'd been going after. A boy, maybe twelve or thirteen. Both the boy and the rescuer were already on the way back to the Pave Hawk. But she wasn't. She was still on the ground, and now she was his mission. He had to rescue the rescuer.

Rafe had to believe if he got to her, that she would

somehow be all right. That he could breathe life into her or do whatever the hell else was needed to fix her and bring her home.

He ran, with the words knifing through his head. *Get to her now!* And his worst enemy wasn't the IEDs or the ones who'd destroyed the building. Not even the ones who were coming for the team and the survivors.

No.

Time was the enemy now.

If he didn't do his job and get to her, then...well, he couldn't go there. Couldn't even consider it.

He'd had the best training possible. This was his prime reason for existing in the military. He was an Air Force Combat Rescue Officer. Now, the bastard enemy of time had to cooperate and let him get to her.

But he could feel every one of those seconds ticking off.

The wind shifted, and suddenly Rafe couldn't see shit. The wall of sand was swallowing him up, blurring his vision and erasing his visual of the extraction. And he figured he had less than a minute before the human enemies closed in. Before his entire team and the extractions all died.

His heartbeat was roaring in his ears now. His pulse was too fast, like those seconds that were ticking away. He'd done rescues like this nearly a hundred times but never with that warning punching him in the gut.

Get to her now!

Rafe pushed forward, his boots bogging down in the sand and his eyes burning. His lungs were on fire. But he finally saw her. Still there, still unmoving.

He didn't check for a pulse or injuries. Not enough time for that. He scooped her up and started running, sprinting with her to the Pave Hawk.

Where she'd get medical treatment.

Where she'd be safe.

But that didn't happen.

The sounds roared through his head, and the pain came. The God-awful, searing pain. And as Rafe fell with her onto the hot sand, he felt, tasted, and smelled his own blood.

Chapter One
———— ☆ ————

Four Years Later

The grimy yellowing bones lay in the makeshift grave.

Rafe Cross stared down at them and fought hard just to catch his breath. He flat-out refused to have one of his flashbacks. Not now. He had to handle it. He had to deal with it, and he couldn't let this sling him back to another place, another time.

Back to hell.

The mental pep talk he was having with himself wasn't as effective as he needed. The muscles in his chest were so tight that they were vising his lungs. He had to keep it together. He couldn't give into the sickening dread that was crawling its way through him.

Tessa.

These were her bones.

She was dead. *She was really dead*.

So, that's where he put his focus. Spelling out the logic of what he was seeing. That would help him process it. And some things fit for this to be her. The general size of the skeleton, even though it was hard for Rafe to tell exactly how tall this dead person would have been.

Then, there was the location, which was only a mile from her home. That fit, too. And the fact that it appeared the bones had been here long enough for the sixteen years

6

that Tessa had been missing.

However, the clincher for this being Tessa was that red leather jacket, the only clothing that hadn't been decomposed in all this time the body had been in the ground. It was custom made with silver wings embroidered on the cuffs. Definitely a unique piece.

For sixteen years, Rafe had believed that Tessa was out there somewhere, living her life. Without him. Yeah, that *without him* part had been a kick to the gut at first. However, that feeling had faded over time because he'd believed that Tessa had turned her back on him and was living it up elsewhere.

But she hadn't been living at all.

Because she was here, in the ground.

Around him, Rafe heard the murmurs of the responders and workers who were no doubt also having to deal with their own shock. The two CSIs, two uniformed deputies from the Canyon Ridge PD, and several members of the work crew who'd unearthed the body about an hour earlier.

Soon, there would be more.

After one of those workers had called 911, things had moved damn fast because Rafe had gotten the call from Tessa's father, Wade Wainwright, shortly thereafter. Since Rafe lived only twenty minutes away, he'd driven straight over. Wade was on the way from a business meeting in Austin and would be arriving any second now.

This was going to bring Wade to his knees.

And it was going to put a lot of others on edge.

Because Tessa hadn't gotten into that grave by herself. She'd been put there either by a killer or someone who'd wanted to conceal her death.

There was another person who would no doubt fall in that "on edge" category. Sheriff Bree O'Neil. Apparently, she, too, was on her way back from a meeting in San Antonio, which was less than an hour away. Bree wouldn't be pleased to see Rafe at her crime scene, so he'd have to deal with that.

"Just an estimate, but I'd say the body's been here for more than a decade, probably closer to two," Rafe heard the medical examiner say.

He was Oliver Barlow. Folks called him Ollie, and he was someone Rafe had known most of his life. Then again, he could say that about many people in the small ranching town of Canyon Ridge. Rafe had moved away when he'd left for college, but basically, he knew anyone over the age of twenty.

Ollie was belly down on the ground, peering into the gaping hole at the remains. "I'll send the body to a forensic anthropologist who can give us a better timeline of when she was put here," Ollie added.

Here was a hole in the ground about thirty yards from an abandoned Victorian-style inn. Not exactly a shallow grave either since it appeared the body had been buried about three feet down. And she might have remained *here* had it not been for a work crew clearing the area so the inn and grounds could be restored by a developer from San Antonio.

One of the workers had discovered the remains and called 911. The dispatcher, who was a close friend of Wade's, had then called him.

Now, the restoration of the inn would be delayed since this was a crime scene. Or rather, a part of one anyway. Rafe had no idea if Tessa had been killed here or if this had been just the site of the body dump. An ideal site to a killer since the inn had been abandoned nearly three decades and was far off the beaten path.

"You're sure the body's female?" Rafe asked Ollie.

"Oh, yeah." Ollie added a firm nod to that. "A wider pelvis and smaller thorax. Dead giveaways for IDing gender." He stopped, cursed. "Sorry. Somebody should probably get me a thesaurus for Christmas so I can learn words that aren't insensitive."

"I'm not sure there are any better words that could make this easier to hear. Or see," Rafe muttered. He cleared his throat and continued. "Any signs of trauma?"

"Yes," Ollie confirmed, but there was hesitation in his voice. "Her skull's been bashed in. Can't tell though if it's post mortem or if it was what killed her." Ollie looked up at him and pointed to his own temple to indicate the specific location.

Since Rafe didn't have a good view of that particular part of the skeleton, he used the stepping stones the CSIs had already set up and went to the other side. Yes, her skull was caved in in all right.

"Could have some from a hard blow," Ollie remarked.

Blunt force trauma. And Rafe's mind began to whirl with the possibilities of that, and he mentally sped right to the worst-case scenarios that would cause something like that. Assuming the worst was the hazards of the job.

Or rather jobs.

For twelve years he'd been special ops in the military. An elite Air Force Combat Rescue Officer, a CRO. When things had gone to hell in a handbasket with that particular career, he'd gotten out of the service to work for a prestigious private consulting group, Maverick Ops.

In both jobs, he'd seen more than his share of dead bodies. And in one case, he'd literally been holding the person when she'd taken her last breath. But Rafe pushed that aside. He couldn't go there and deal with this, too.

One shitstorm trauma at a time.

"I don't see any obvious defensive wounds," Ollie went on a moment later as he fanned a flashlight over the remains. Even though it was early afternoon and there was plenty of spring sunshine, there were some dark areas in the grave. "No broken fingers or gashes to any of the bones on the hands. Of course, with no tissue, I can't tell if there were cuts or bruises at the time of her death."

Again, that vised his lungs, and Rafe had to mutter a reminder for him to breathe. His body had to understand he wasn't in combat. There would be no sprinting through the desert to save someone.

Because this person was past the point of being rescued.

Ollie got to his feet, dusting off his gloved hands, and faced him. Since Ollie was nearly six feet tall, he didn't have to look too far up at Rafe to get direct eye contact, only a couple of inches, and Rafe immediately saw the mix of emotions in the ME's expression. A mix that took Rafe a moment to interpret.

Hell.

Did Ollie believe he'd killed Tessa?

Rafe didn't get a chance to set him straight because there was the roar of an engine. Emphasis on roar and the equally noisy stop of brakes jarring to a stop on the narrow driveway that fronted the inn.

Wade.

Rafe looked over his shoulder at the massive, barrel-chested man with the sugar-white Stetson that was the identical color of his hair. In a blink, Wade was out of his silver truck and hurrying toward them.

"Is it her?" Wade shouted. "Is it my baby girl?"

Baby girl.

The term struck Rafe as both sad and endearing. Tessa had been twenty-two when she'd disappeared, and if alive, she'd be the same age as Rafe. Thirty-eight. But technically she would always be Wade's baby girl since she was his only child.

"Is it Tessa?" Wade demanded with both the volume and the panic rising in his voice. He had his attention pinned to Rafe.

"We don't know," Rafe said, stepping in front of Wade to keep him from charging right into the burial pit.

That didn't relieve one ounce of the tension that was coming off Wade in thick, hot waves. "The worker said there was a red jacket."

"There is, but we don't know if it's Tessa," Rafe insisted. "She'll have to be examined before we know for sure."

Wade shook his head, the tears already welling in his dust-gray eyes, and he made another attempt to bolt to the grave. Rafe was no lightweight, but Wade outsized him by a good fifty pounds. Plus, there was all that fierce determination of a father to see his child. No way to battle that, and Wade managed to get close enough to the edge to look down at the bones.

A hoarse wail tore from Wade's throat. It sounded more animal than human. Pure primal grief that seemed to rip through every part of him. And Rafe had been right. Wade dropped to his knees.

"My baby," Wade sobbed. "My beautiful baby girl."

Rafe stooped down and reached to take hold of Wade's shoulders to anchor him and stop him from falling face-first onto the ground, but the man fell into his arms instead, burying his face on Rafe's shoulder. Wade cried a flow of tears that seemed endless.

Rafe didn't even attempt any questions. Though he had plenty. Specifically, he wanted to know the last time

Wade had heard from Tessa. Rafe knew about one long text that'd come shortly after she'd disappeared.

That one had been an apology of sorts, a "this town is just too small for me" sentiment.

Rafe had gotten a nearly identical one that'd crushed what was left of his twenty-two-year-old heart. That was his one and only correspondence from Tessa, but Rafe remembered about a year later that Wade had called to say he'd received another text, and in it, Tessa had assured him she was all right and happy.

Had Tessa already been dead by then?

If so, the texts could have come from her killer.

And then there were the questions he had about Tessa's trust fund. Tessa had come from money. Plenty of it. Specifically, her father's and late mother's money, which, from all accounts, were both sizeable.

About three months after Tessa's disappearance, Wade had said that a large chunk of money—about a half million dollars—had been electronically withdrawn from Tessa's trust fund. If Tessa hadn't done that, then that was something else that could lead back to the killer.

Rafe's mind was already whirling with the possible threads of a murder investigation when there was the sound of another approaching vehicle. A Canyon Ridge PD cruiser. It got Wade's attention as well because he lifted his head and aimed his gaze at the brunette woman in the dark blue uniform who stepped out.

Sheriff Bree O'Neil.

She was on the tall side for a woman. A solid five nine, and she still had a runner's athletic body that had earned her a state championship in cross country back when they'd been in high school. Her hair had changed though. She no longer had the ponytail that swished back and forth when she ran but now wore it short and with a choppy cut.

When they'd been eight, Tessa, Bree, and he had become blood friends. A variation of blood brothers, but it had involved cutting themselves and going through the ritual of smearing that blood on each other's wounds. It had also ended up with Tessa needing some stitches since she'd cut a little too deep in the wrong place on her wrist. She'd been damn lucky she hadn't bled to death.

That memory came to a full-fledged mental stop because clearly Tessa hadn't gotten so lucky after all.

But in those days, Tessa had been someone that people talked about. Oh, how she could light up a room, folks said. So beautiful, so full of energy. The flip side to that was the self-absorption that had surfaced in her teens. And the occasional stinging remarks Tessa aimed at those who didn't have the fastest cars or the finest clothes.

From all accounts, that mean streak had gained some serious traction after her mother's death when Tessa had been twenty-two. Then, Tessa had simply vanished.

Rafe yanked his focus back to Bree, who was now doing a cop's sweep, glancing around the grounds. She no doubt thought this was a damn creepy place, what with the crumbling mansion with its paint-scabbed exterior and the overgrown gardens littered with weeds. Littered, too, with blank milky-eyed marble statues that seemed ready to charge at them like an army from hell.

Even from the twenty feet of distance that separated them, Rafe noted the deep breath Bree took and the dread on her face. Dread for what she knew she was about to see with those bones. But then her gaze shifted to him, and he thought she muttered some profanity under her breath.

Yeah, she was not going to like a consultant on her crime scene.

Maverick Ops had a stellar reputation for having the vast resources and top-notch personnel to solve hard cases that baffled law enforcement. Also, for rescuing kidnapped victims and providing personal security with trained bodyguards and equipment. That made them heroes in the various communities when victims finally got some hard justice.

Cops didn't have that same opinion of them though.

Most cops tended to see consultants as renegades who cut corners. Corners they themselves couldn't cut because their hands were legally tied because of the badges they wore.

The cops were right.

But Rafe always thought the bottom line was what mattered most. And the bottom line for him was that justice was worth cutting the occasional corners. It was worth pretty much everything, and it was a damn pisser of a bitter pill to swallow when that justice never came.

Ready to do some verbal sparring with his childhood friend, AKA the sheriff, Rafe stood from his stooping position while also easing Wade back to his feet. He kept a steadying arm around him though, in case the man tried to climb in the grave with what was left of his baby girl. Wade didn't move though. He stayed put while Bree made her way toward them.

"It's Tessa," Wade blurted, the grief so thick in his voice that it was barely a whisper.

Bree looked at Ollie and her two deputies, Alice Wright and Carson Mendoza, for verification. Alice nodded. Carson lifted his shoulder in a noncommittal shrug. Ollie did pretty much the same. Only then did Bree shift back to Rafe, maybe looking for a tiebreaker verdict.

Rafe went with a noncommittal response as well. "It could be Tessa," he settled for saying.

Bree made a sound that could have meant anything. Or nothing. And staying on the CSI stepstones as well, she made her way closer, peering into the grave.

Because Rafe was watching her so closely, he saw the muscles flicker in her jaw. Heard her swallow hard. Some of the color drained from her face.

She stood there a moment, obviously trying to steel herself up from the shock. As he'd done, Bree was probably reliving some of that mountain of memories the three of them had made for the first twenty-two years of their lives.

Not all good memories, of course.

Not with Tessa's often high-maintenance personality.

But at the moment, it was memories about the living, breathing woman who'd once been their blood friend.

"Could I have a word with you," Bree said, motioning for Rafe to follow her. It wasn't a question.

"I called him," Wade spoke up, clearly aware of the potential pissing contest that might be about to happen. "I want him here. He loved Tessa, and he'll find out who did this to my baby girl."

Yes, he had indeed loved her. Probably not so much during those last days when she'd been trying to talk Rafe out of going into the military. But once, there'd been love. And sex since Tessa and he had been each other's firsts. Wade probably didn't want to know that though.

"Keep an eye on Wade," Rafe muttered to Ollie, and the ME immediately took Wade by the arm and began leading him away from the grave. Away from Bree and Rafe as well.

Bree made another of those sounds that meant exactly squat and started walking toward her cruiser. Rafe followed, and he didn't even launch into an argument as to why he should be here.

But he wasn't sure he should be.

Wade had called him in and wanted him on scene. However, Rafe had learned the hard way—the *really* hard way—that a personal involvement with the victim meant zero objectivity. Lack of objectivity was a good way to screw things up and get people killed.

Yeah, lesson learned about that.

"Before today, did you know that Tessa was dead?" Bree asked him the moment they were out of earshot of the others.

"No. And I didn't kill her," he tacked onto that.

Bree's head whipped up, her gaze spearing his, and something flitted across her face. Hurt, maybe? "I know that," she muttered. She paused and then repeated it while she shook her head.

A heavy silence settled between them for a couple of moments before he saw the shift in Bree's posture. She was the cop again now, and this was her crime scene. One she could handle if she could put aside the personal history between Tessa and her. After all, Bree wasn't a rookie. She'd been a police officer for eighteen years, first as a deputy and then as the sheriff when her father had retired from the position.

"Who called this in?" she asked. Definitely all cop now. "Which one found the body?"

"Gavin McCray," Rafe provided, thumbing back through the mental notes that he'd made from his phone call with Wade and his brief conversations with Ollie and the deputies. "He's not local so you probably won't know him. He's with a work crew from San Antonio."

Rafe glanced through the group so he could point to the beefy backhoe operator who'd been wearing a hard hat and muddy overalls. But he wasn't there. Rafe was about to expand his visual search to the area near the portable toilet and the other equipment.

When the explosion ripped through the air.
And all hell broke loose.

Chapter Two

———— ☆ ————

Bree heard the deafening blast and had the sensation of all the air being sucked out of her lungs.

Right before she went airborne.

Her back slammed against the cruiser door. Hard. So hard that she stood no chance of gathering her breath any time soon. And the pain shot through her. A bone-jarring pain that she could feel in every part of her body.

God, what had happened?

She slid from the cruiser to the ground, automatically reaching for her Glock 19 in her shoulder holster to try to fight whatever threat was happening. Bree managed to draw the gun, too, and from the corner of her eye, she saw that Rafe had pulled out his weapon as well. A Sig-Sauer that he must have had in a concealed holster.

"Explosion," he said.

Bree's ears were ringing so she couldn't actually hear the word, but she saw it form on his lips. Lips that were bleeding. Rafe had a cut on the side of his mouth. Another on his forehead, and he looked as if he had also been slammed against the cruiser.

"Explosion," she repeated, hoping by saying it, it would help her make sense of things.

It didn't. But glancing around clarified a whole lot.

Oh, shit.

Her deputies were down on the ground. So were Ollie, Wade, the CSIs, and the worker she'd seen when she had first driven up. They were all moving though and probably making the same moaning sounds of pain that she was.

Leaning against the cruiser for support, Bree managed to get to her feet. Not easily. And beside her, Rafe was struggling to do that as well. Struggling some more to take out his phone, and she saw he was calling 911, requesting an ambulance. Something she would have thought to do if she'd had just another second or two to gather her thoughts.

Gulping in some much needed air, she fired glances around while she began to make her way to the wounded. Each step was a challenge, and while she didn't think anything was broken, she'd have bruises and plenty of aches from being tossed through the air like a ragdoll.

Somehow, Rafe got ahead of her, moving straight to the two CSIs who'd been right by the grave the last time she'd looked. Bree aimed for her deputies who'd been further to the right of it. Carson Mendoza was already on his feet and had similar injuries to Rafe. Alice, however, was still on the ground.

Both Carson and Bree converged on Alice, easing her over onto her back so Bree could check for a pulse. She was alive, thank heaven, but she had a lot more blood on her than Carson and Rafe. Than Ollie and Wade, too, who'd been even further away from the grave than the deputies. The two of them were already standing as well and looking shellshocked at the carnage in front of them.

"I think my leg's broken," Alice muttered, and wincing and groaning, she tried to lever herself up on her elbows. Carson and Bree helped with that while Bree continued to glance around, looking for more injured.

And for the cause of what'd just happened.

Bree saw the gaping hole in the ground. Not the grave. She wasn't sure it was even still there, but if so, it was buried under the debris from...what? A bomb? Dynamite?

No.

She drew in a long breath and smelled something.

"Is there a gas line out here?" she asked no one in particular.

"There is," someone answered. A big guy in a hard hat. This had to be Gavin McCray, the one who'd found the body. "But it's not supposed to be active. My crew boss checked with the utility company before I started digging."

Clearly, Bree would be having a chat with the boss. And with the utility company. For now though, they had to get out of there in case there was another explosion.

"We have to move," Bree insisted, but she debated it as she said it.

If Alice had internal injuries, moving her could make things worse. It could kill her. But so could a secondary blast, and Bree thought the smell of gas was getting stronger.

"Use this," Rafe said, dragging over a blue tarp that he yanked off a piece of equipment.

Again, he moved fast, spreading it out next to Alice

while he murmured to the deputy. Clearly, this wasn't his first rodeo when it came to tending wounded, and Bree figured he'd done such things when he'd been an Air Force Combat Rescue Officer.

"You're going to be all right," Rafe said to Alice. He lifted her eyelid, checking the response of her pupil. "Tell me where you're hurting."

"My leg," Alice was quick to say, and the pain coated her voice. "My shoulder, too."

"Anything hurting in your ribs or stomach?" Rafe asked.

Wincing, Alice shook her head. "I don't think so."

"Good. I'm going to ease you onto the tarp," Rafe explained.

Rafe looked up at Bree, motioning for her to take Alice's feet. She did that while he took the deputy's torso. Even though they tried to be gentle, Alice still cried out in pain.

It tore at Bree to hear Alice make that sound. To see her cut up like this. To see this nightmare. One that she knew could be much worse if they didn't get away from what was left of that gas pipe.

Rafe and she carried Alice on the tarp, placing the deputy on the other side of the cruiser where she'd at least be protected if there was indeed another blast. The others followed suit, all hobbling their way toward cover.

In the distance, Bree heard the welcome sound of an ambulance siren. Soon, Alice would get the medical treatment she needed. The rest of the wounded would, too. But while they waited and while Rafe continued to talk to Alice, Bree made a call to the emergency dispatcher to get out more ambulances, the fire department and some experts to check the gas line.

There wasn't a fire at the moment, but it was possible the gas would ignite one, and she wanted the firemen there in case that happened. Added to that, she needed more help in securing the scene and keeping people out, and she might not have the manpower to do that.

"If you can, move to the deputies' cruiser," Bree instructed Wade, Ollie, and the construction workers.

Since they were all up and somewhat mobile, that seemed the safest option and would put them even further from the initial blast.

"What do you want me to do?" Carson asked.

His hands were trembling. That was the first time Bree had ever seen him have that reaction, and they'd worked together for more than a dozen years. Then again, it wasn't exactly a common occurrence to find a body and nearly be blown to bits all in the same hour.

"Get the contact info for the workers," Bree instructed. "And arrange for them to be checked by EMTs after Alice is transported to the hospital. You're sure you're okay?" she tacked onto that when Carson rubbed his arm.

Carson nodded, and that's when she also noticed the blood on his head. His thick black hair had initially concealed it, but she could see it now. She took hold of his hand and eased him to a sitting position next to Alice and Rafe.

"The contact info can wait," Bree amended. "You need to be examined, too."

Hell, all of them needed to be. Her ribs were starting to throb.

Since her own legs were far from steady, Bree sat down on the ground, trying to get her mind to settle enough so she could think straight. Rafe didn't seem to be having that problem. He had already moved to check Carson for injuries.

Despite not being in an actual uniform but rather dark jeans and a black t-shirt, Rafe looked very much like the military special ops officer he'd been. His moves were quick and efficient. No sign of nerves or hesitation whatsoever despite nearly being killed.

"You must have been good at your job as a Combat Rescue Officer," Bree heard herself say.

Rafe looked at her, their gazes colliding. And that's when she realized he wasn't quite as steady as his quick reactions had led her to believe. He was dragging in some long breaths, and she thought he might be fighting off a panic attack.

PTSD, maybe?

"Flashbacks," he said as if reading her mind. "I'll be okay." And it sounded as if he was trying to convince himself of that.

"Definitely good at your job," she repeated. Because

despite this having shaken him to the core, he was holding it together.

"Sometimes, I was good at it," he answered after a long pause. "If you ever need rescuing, there's an eighty percent chance I'll be successful." It seemed he added that last bit as an attempt to make things lighter.

"Good to know," she muttered. "And the other twenty percent?" Bree had to ask.

Something went through his cool green eyes. Something dark and not so cool. "The other twenty percent is the reason I'm here and not there."

More darkness. There was definitely an old wound just underneath the surface. She couldn't recall hearing any near misses or horror stories about Rafe's time in the service. Then again, what he did had likely been classified and didn't make headlines or reach the gossips.

The sound of the sirens got closer, and she shifted her attention as the first of the ambulances pulled to a stop in between the two cruisers. Bree got to her feet, motioning for the EMTs to head her way. They did, though both did some gawking at the scene sprawled out in front of them.

Rafe and Bree stepped back to let the EMTs get to Alice and Carson, and since the deputies were now in good hands, Bree and he made their way to the others who were huddled together about ten yards away. Before she reached them, her phone dinged with a text.

"The gas company is sending out an inspector," Bree relayed to Rafe as she continued to read the message.

"Apparently, the gas was turned off here years ago."

"So, the gas company is wrong. or else someone tampered with it," Rafe said. "Or someone used a form of gas in the IED that went off."

Yes. Those were her conclusions, too. Of course, there was the possibility this was some kind of fluke accident, that maybe the gas line had leaked enough to cause this. But that theory didn't feel right. It especially didn't feel right, considering the blast had likely destroyed most of the remains.

"More ambulances are on the way," Bree called out as Rafe and she approached the group by the deputies' cruiser.

And she could see the EMTs were going to be busy. One of the CSIs had blood spilling down the side of his head. A worker was cradling either an injured or broken arm.

"What the hell happened here?" Wade asked. His head was bleeding as well, and Ollie had his hand pressed against it to try to staunch the flow.

"I'm not sure," Bree admitted. "But trust me, it'll be investigated."

"And my baby girl's body?" Wade added. "What about her?" His voice cracked on the last word as his attention drifted toward what was left of the grave.

"It'll be investigated," Bree repeated, wishing she could give him more.

There was another wail of sirens. And even though every moment seemed like an eternity, the fire engine and another ambulance finally pulled into the driveway. As the first EMTs had done, the responders barreled out of their vehicles. Two EMTs and three firemen, which she knew was the entire day shift.

"Tend to them," Bree instructed the EMTs, pointing to Ollie, Wade, the CSIs, and the workers. She motioned for the fire chief, Davy Werner, to step aside with her. "The gas company is sending someone out, but I'd like this whole area evacuated, including the ranches that are within a quarter of a mile of here. Can you and your crew help with that?"

"Absolutely," Davy was quick to agree, and he opened his mouth to say something else, stopped and shook his head. "Hell, Bree. It looks like a damn warzone out here. And I heard somebody found Tessa Wainwright's body."

Bree sighed, hating that word like that was already going around, but gossip was fast in a small ranching town. Especially gossip about a woman who'd once been prom queen, cheerleader, and most likely to succeed all in one.

Tessa had also been Rafe's girlfriend.

His lover. And Bree needed to make sure she remembered that when they spoke. She'd need to tread lightly in case he still had feelings for Tessa.

She would need to tread lightly with herself, too. Because, well, there were her own old residual feelings for Rafe. Ones that he thankfully never knew about. There was already enough awkwardness between them without adding that.

"It's possibly Tessa," Bree muttered, but then she stopped as well. "There was a red leather jacket on the remains."

Davy's head whipped toward her. "With silver angel wings on the cuffs?"

She nodded. Sighed again. Of course, Davy would recall that. It'd been a staple in Tessa's wardrobe, and she'd worn it everywhere, including during the summer when it'd been hotter than hell.

"We've got binoculars on the truck," Davy went on a moment later. "Let me get them and see if I can spot anyone or anything. You've accounted for everyone that was on scene?"

"Yes." And she counted them off for good measure. "Three workers, two CSIs, two deputies, Wade, Ollie, the workers, Rafe and me."

That caused Davy's head to whip up again, and he turned, no doubt looking for Rafe. Prom king, star quarterback, and the most likely to succeed partner to Tessa. The term, *charmed life*, had fit both Tessa and him.

Yet, here they were. With Tessa likely dead and Rafe with that dark, haunted look in his eyes.

"Hell, I didn't notice Rafe when I drove up," Davy remarked. "Not a good time to catch up with him though. Let me get the binoculars." With that, he hurried back toward the truck.

Bree took out her phone and texted dispatch to light a fire under the gas line inspector to get him or her out here

ASAP. She'd just hit send when she looked up and saw Rafe making his way back to her.

"How bad are the injuries?" she immediately asked.

"I don't think anyone is critical. It seems your deputies and the two CSIs got the worst of it."

She had to agree, and if they all managed to get out of this with broken bones, concussions, and such, then they were lucky.

"If the blast had happened just minutes earlier, we would have likely been killed," Bree muttered.

"Probably. We were all standing around the grave. The only reason I moved away is because you wanted that word with me. The others moved back a little after we left."

Yes, they had, and that caused a knot to form in her stomach. She glanced at Gavin McCray again, the worker who was now being treated by an EMT. The worker who'd found the body, called it in, and then was seemingly nowhere in sight when the explosion happened.

"Yeah," Rafe muttered, and that's when Bree realized he'd followed her gaze and knew she was looking at Gavin. "You'll want to do a deep dive into his background."

She would indeed and would start that as soon as she got back to the office. Normally, she'd tap one of the deputies for a background check like that, but with both day deputies here and hurt, it would have to wait. As it was, dispatch was already having to bring in one of the swing shift deputies just to cover the office.

"Do you have any experience with explosions?" she

asked, watching as Davy started surveying the scene with the binoculars. Since she wanted her own look, she started in that direction, with Rafe following right alongside her.

"Some," Rafe answered.

Even though his expression didn't change, she heard something in his voice. Maybe something to do with that twenty percent who hadn't gotten rescued.

Rafe stopped just a few feet from Davy and motioned to the left of where the grave had been. "I think that's the point of origin for the blast."

She saw the mound of displaced dirt and debris, and if that was indeed where the explosion had gone off, it was only about two yards from the grave.

"I see bones," Davy said, drawing her attention back to him, and both Rafe and she hurried to join him. "They're scattered, but I can make out at least three."

Davy passed her the binoculars, and while it took her a moment to focus and find the right spot, she did indeed see bones.

And something else.

Something...

"Oh, God," Bree managed, and she immediately passed the binoculars to Rafe, hoping she was wrong.

She had to be wrong.

Rafe pressed the binoculars to his eyes, moved around. And cursed.

"Hell, there's a body out there," Rafe confirmed. "Not a skeleton. *A body*."

Chapter Three

——— ☆ ———

Rafe stood at the far back corner of Bree's office at Canyon Ridge PD, while she was on the phone. This time, getting an update from the gas company.

Before that, there had been calls to Davy at the fire department and the hospital to check on the wounded. And before that, Bree had fielded calls from the mayor and members of the town council who had wanted to be certain that pipelines all over town weren't going to explode.

She had given all of them the reassurance, along with some for her father, too, who'd called her after someone in town had let him know about the troubles going on.

Bree had had to do some fast talking to prevent her father from coming back from a month-long European vacation. A much needed one from all accounts with Bree's mom, her brother and sister-in-law. Even though Rafe was certain Bree could have indeed used her father's help, she had convinced him not to cut the vacation short, that she could handle things.

Rafe had listened to Bree dole out all those attempts to comfort and soothe. Had heard the fatigue and stress in her voice. But Bree had held strong, giving out what was actually very little info as to what had happened.

Yes, it was likely Tessa's body.

Yes, there'd been a blast.

Yes, there'd been another body that was yet to be identified.

Rafe was working on all of that and more, but this was the stage of the investigation where there was a flood of info, and he wasn't sure what was useful and what was white noise. Still, he'd gotten his own reports on the injured. Ollie, Wade, the construction workers, and both CSIs had already been treated and released.

The two deputies were a different matter.

Both had concussions, serious ones, and Alice did indeed have a broken leg and a dislocated shoulder. Carson had two broken ribs and had needed stitches for the gash on his head. Rafe wasn't expecting either of the deputies to return to duty, which left Bree and the two off-shift cops she'd called in.

They were drowning in that flood of info, but so far, Bree hadn't asked him to help. And wouldn't. Well, not unless she got desperate, and it very well might come to that.

Especially once they had an ID on the other body.

Rafe had been looking into that angle as well, and he'd asked his boss, Ruby Maverick, to find out what she could. Ruby was retired special ops, but she also had a knack for hacking.

Something Bree definitely wouldn't approve of.

Of course, nothing learned from the hacking would hold up in court. But Rafe wasn't looking for the letter of the law here. He wanted an ID since that info could blow this case wide open.

He listened to the side of Bree's phone conversation he could hear, with the CSIs this time, and he drank more of what had to be the worst coffee he'd ever had in his life. And that was saying something since he'd had some bad stuff. He figured it was eating away at the lining of his stomach, but he needed it.

Bad.

The adrenaline had long since come and gone in the three hours since the explosion, leaving him with a familiar bone-deep exhaustion.

One that he couldn't do anything about.

He sure as hell wasn't going home, not until he had some answers about Tessa, that other body, and the blast. Bree clearly felt the same way because once they'd been given a somewhat hesitant clearance from the EMTs, she'd come straight to her office to get started on the investigation.

Bree hadn't exactly invited him to come along, but Rafe had invited himself. Besides, he'd needed to give his statement of the incident, and since there hadn't been an available deputy to do that, he'd written it himself.

Like Bree, he was getting constant updates, too, that he'd requested from his boss, including a report on Gavin McCray that Ruby had just texted him. So far, there was nothing to indicate the construction worker could be a killer, but it was early yet.

Things surfaced.

So far though, nada. Gavin had no criminal record and had worked for the construction company for nearly six years. An unblemished record and all that. He was married and had four kids, all under the age of eight. The man had no savings and was living right on the edge financially, and that could make him vulnerable to some things.

Murder? Blowing shit up? Attempting to destroy evidence?

Maybe.

It would require further digging, along with hearing what the man had to say once he was in interview. That might not happen for a while though since Gavin had apparently slipped out from the hospital and gone home.

Bree had nearly blown a few gaskets about that, but there'd literally been no one to keep an eye on all the people and all the moving parts of this investigation. So, Bree had called Gavin and had insisted he come into the station to give a statement.

The next report Rafe read, also from Ruby, was about the gas line. It had definitely been turned off, and there was no indication it had been turned back on, either legally or by someone hoping to obstruct justice. Rafe didn't know Ruby's source for that info, but it'd be reliable. Everything about the woman was.

And it was the reason Rafe worked for her.

According to Ruby, the initial indications were the explosion had indeed had a gas source, but that it'd been a device set up near the grave. No details yet on the type of device, how long it'd been there, and how or why it'd been detonated, but Ruby would no doubt be digging to get those answers.

Bree finished her talk with the CSIs, sighed, and her fingers hovered over her phone screen as if she were about to make another call. She finally muttered something he didn't catch, set down her phone, and chugged the rest of her own coffee. The grimace she made led him to believe they had the same opinion of the godawful brew.

"The unidentified body is on the way to Ollie," she stated. "What's left of the bones from the grave are being gathered. But the county only has part-time use of a forensic anthropologist, and he can't get to the bones for another month. The town council has approved the budget to contract out."

She looked at him then, and Rafe knew where this was leading. "Maverick Ops has a forensic anthropologist on staff."

"Yeah," she grumbled as if she'd known that would be his response and wasn't especially pleased about it. "Normally, something like this wouldn't be funded, but...well, Wade. And Wade didn't ask for any favors, by the way. But the members of the town council figure that's because he's in shock, and they want to get answers for him as to whether or not the bones belong to Tessa."

Rafe made a sound of agreement and fired off a text to Ruby to give her a heads-up about the request she'd soon be getting. "Wade and Ruby are friends, and Ruby will offer up whatever's needed," he concluded.

Bree didn't actually say anything, but Rafe figured he knew what she was thinking. Wade wasn't the only one who'd had money. So had Rafe's parents before they'd both been killed a decade ago in a private plane crash. His folks hadn't quite been as well off as Wade, but Rafe had heard the "to the manor born" remarks about both Tessa and him.

No manor birth for Bree. Her father had been the sheriff, and her mom, a school teacher. Still, they both carried the faint scar from the blood friends' bond.

And carried other things, too.

Like the coffee, the timing equally sucked for him to recall that once Bree had had a crush on him. She hadn't acted on it, of course. No poaching on a blood friend's guy. But the attraction had been there.

It hadn't been one sided either.

Rafe had had his own crush on her. Unlike Bree though—he had seen the heat for him in her eyes—but he believed he'd managed to keep his feelings for her a secret.

"My boss is standing by for your request for the forensic anthropologist," he relayed when he got a response back from Ruby.

She nodded, muttered a thanks, and then groaned while she scrubbed her hand over her face. Bree didn't say anything until she'd gotten up and closed the door. It wasn't especially loud in the squad room, but there were some townsfolk there, talking to the deputies, and she obviously wanted to keep what she had to say to him private.

But Rafe believed he already knew.

"The town council didn't just spring for the bone specialist but also for additional help for you," he spelled out to her. "They want me to assist and for you to agree to the assistance."

She wouldn't be very good at poker, not with her usual tell of a tightening jaw muscle. Bree sighed. Then gave an equally tight nod.

"And, of course, Wade's friends on the town council want you and are willing to pay you out of pocket." She paused. "You really earn as much as I've heard?"

"I'm not sure what you've heard—"

"Ten grand a day plus expenses," she interrupted.

Now, he sighed. "Yeah. Private consulting and security usually have clients with big budgets."

"Like Wade's friends on the town council," she muttered, making that sound like profanity.

And in her mind, it was. Wade's friends were tossing around their money and interfering with her investigation. But the way Rafe saw it, she needed an extra hand or two.

"I'll waive my fee and expenses for this," Rafe let her know right up front. "You're short of manpower, and I can help." But then he stopped. *Maybe* he could help.

Hell, could he?

Or was he so damn close to this that he'd screw it up?

"Yes," she said, obviously picking up on his hesitation.

Rafe wished his hesitation about his involvement in this would rein him in and at least make him think twice about consulting. But it wouldn't. That explosion had dragged him into this, and he was staying. Well, staying if Bree let him. Wade and his friends might have money and influence, but she had the badge.

She stared at him for some snail-crawling moments, and he had no trouble reading her expression. Resignation. He saw it. And felt it in himself, too.

Yes, they'd be on this together.

"You've been texting and reading replies since we got here," Bree commented, clearly shifting gears. "Do you have anything that'll help make sense of this?"

Using his phone, he fired off copies of Ruby's emails to Bree. "Those are preliminary reports from the gas company and the initial assessment of what caused the explosion. There's also the deep dive on Gavin McCray."

Her mouth went into a flat line, and her amber-brown eyes narrowed a bit. Still, she opened the reports. "Ten grand a day," Bree grumbled. "I don't make nearly that in a month."

"Then, you're way underpaid."

He had to stop himself from adding a sales pitch for her to join the Maverick Ops team. Bree wasn't former military, a preference of Ruby's, but there were a couple of other non-vets in the group.

"Look, my specialty isn't crime scene investigation," he spelled out for her. "I'm Maverick Ops' search and rescue guy. But we do have a former investigator on the team. He's ex-military, an agent for the Air Force Office of Special Investigation, which is sort of like FBI. He was also raised by hardcore doomsday preppers so he's, well, resourceful when needed. His name is Jericho McKenna."

Her head whipped up. "The guy who solved those four cold case serial killings in Waco?" she asked.

Rafe nodded. The case had made national news, along with making Jericho somewhat of a celebrity. Rafe and the other team members made sure Jericho got a whole lot of ribbing about that, too, including the mock *Sexiest Man Alive* magazine cover they'd had done up for Jericho. That was after he'd gotten fan mail from women who wanted to marry him and have his babies.

"I doubt even the town council would spring for a second consultant," she admitted. Again, she made the word *consultant* sound like something down and dirty. "Wade's town council friends want you because they believe your love for Tessa will make you work hard to find justice for her."

"I *will* work hard," he verified. He shouldn't have paused. And he sure as hell shouldn't have added, "But I haven't loved Tessa for a very long time."

Bree studied him as if looking for an obvious lie. She wouldn't see one because it was the truth.

Finally, she nodded and opened the reports Rafe had forwarded to her. Her jaw did more tightening as she read them.

"You think Gavin McCray could have had something to do with this?" Bree came out and asked.

"Possibly. *Possibly*," he emphasized, "and it's a thread that'll obviously need to be tied off. I can ask my boss to put some boots on the ground to subtly question Gavin's friends and work associates."

Bree looked ready to nip that in the bud, but then she nodded. "I want to close this fast. If there's a killer out there, I want him or her caught and tossed in jail."

The silence came, settling like dead weight between them, before Rafe broke it. "The inn isn't on any of the main roads, which was likely the reason it went out of business."

She nodded, and while she no doubt had already come to the same conclusion, it was clearly eating away at him. "Which means the killer is probably local." Bree stopped, cursed. "Which means we have to dig through every detail of Tessa's past. Your past," she tacked onto that.

"In part," Rafe agreed. "But after we all left for college, Tessa must have seen other men." He mentally took out the *must have*. She had, period. "Tessa and I hooked up in high school, yes, but you're probably aware we drifted apart while I was at A&M and she was in Austin at UT."

Yeah, Bree was aware all right even though she'd attended college in San Antonio. It might have been less than a two-hour drive between College Station where A&M was located and where Tessa was attending the University of Texas, but at most Tessa and he managed a night or two per semester and during the holidays. Then, it became even less than that once Tessa had realized she wasn't going to be able to talk him out of going into special ops in the Air Force.

"Don't put your *boots on the ground* consultants onto a deep dive into Tessa," Bree insisted, going with the lingo he'd used. "We'll do that one." She continued to look at him, probably trying to see if it was going to bother him when they learned Tessa had been with other men.

It wouldn't.

Rafe didn't get a chance to vocalize that though because Bree continued before he could speak. "I'm guessing we need Tessa's DNA to compare to the bones. It's not on file," she quickly let him know. "That leaves maybe getting it from a hairbrush or something personal."

"Or from Wade," he said, and Rafe wished this was something he'd already told her about.

Then again, they'd had a lot going on since the explosion.

"Wade's head was bleeding while he was waiting to be tended to by the EMTs, and he used his handkerchief to wipe the blood," Rafe explained. "He threw it into the trash, but I asked him if I could put it in an evidence bag that I got from one of the EMTs."

Oh, yeah. He should have found a way to tell her this sooner.

"And?" she prompted, her mouth set in a hard frown.

"And Wade agreed, though I think he was too dazed to realize what it would be used for. Then, while you were busy with your deputies, I had a courier pick it up to take it to my boss."

Clearly, he was going to have to add to this and spell out that he didn't have authorization to send it to the county lab. Nor had he wanted to do that since it would have taken days or even weeks to process.

There was also the issue of the chain of custody on the handkerchief. The bottom line—it wouldn't have been admissible if needed in court, but then if admissibility had truly played into this, Bree or one of her deputies would have had to take the sample or at least supervise that being done.

Bree drew in a long breath and squeezed her eyes shut a moment. "Wade had thrown the handkerchief away?" she clarified.

Rafe nodded. That technically absolved him of any wrongdoing. Technically. Trash was considered fair game for cops and other investigators.

"I'll tell Wade about sending it for DNA analysis once he's had a little while to absorb all of this," Rafe added.

Bree would have no doubt had plenty to say about that, but her phone rang. She glanced at it and muttered something he didn't catch.

"It's Ollie," she relayed, and this time, she put the call on speaker.

Apparently, she'd accepted that they'd be working together and that he needed to be privy to whatever could help with the investigation.

"Ollie," she answered and immediately added, "You're on speaker. Rafe is here and listening in."

"Are you two okay?" Ollie asked after a short pause.

"Fine. Some bruises, that's all," Bree explained. "And you?"

"Some bruises and a few butterfly bandages on some cuts." He paused again. "I'm at my office, and I figured you were, too. Are you ready to talk business, or would you rather wait—"

"Business," she interrupted. "Do you have something?"

"Yes. Two things actually. I just did an initial exam of the body recovered from the crime scene. Female. Mid to late thirties. Blonde hair, blue eyes. I don't recognize her, but then there was a lot of damage to her face from the explosion."

"Did she die in the blast?" Rafe quickly asked.

"No. Full rigor mortis had set in, so I'm guessing she'd been dead anywhere from eight to twenty-three hours. I'll be able to narrow that down more with some tests. Can't give you cause of death either right now because I've got to figure out which of her injuries are post-mortem."

"The CSIs haven't found any indication she was killed at the site," Bree offered. "Then again, it's possible she was, and the explosion obliterated any potential evidence. There isn't much left of the crime scene."

"True, but both the CSIs and I took photos shortly after we arrived, and we have those. I've been looking at them," Ollie muttered. "I'm going to put a big-assed question mark next to what I'm about to say because I could be wrong."

"Wrong? About what?" Bree asked.

"The photos of the skeletal remains," Ollie provided, and Rafe heard the man take in a deep breath. "I'm not sure these remains are Tessa's."

Chapter Four

———— ☆ ————

"What?" Bree couldn't get that out fast enough, and she mentally repeated what Ollie had just said to make sure she'd heard him right.

She had.

Rafe was clearly doing some silent questioning as well. His forehead was bunched up, and his eyes had gone intense.

"Why do you think the remains aren't Tessa's?" Rafe asked when Ollie didn't add anything else.

"It's all speculation at this point...look, why don't the two of you come over to the morgue, and I'll show you what I mean? That'll be better than trying to explain it to you over the phone. That way, you can have a look at the pictures for yourself and can decide if you're seeing the same thing I am."

"We're on the way," Bree said, grabbing her keys and already heading out of her office door. "See you in about five minutes," she added to Ollie.

Maybe less than that since the morgue was in the back part of the hospital, and it was only about a quarter of a mile away from the police station. Normally, Bree would have walked that short distance, but she didn't want to be stopped by anyone along the way to be asked about the investigation and the explosion. She didn't have enough answers yet to have to deal with that.

Rafe was right behind her as she passed through the squad room. "We're on our way to see the medical examiner," she told Deputy Millie Hernadez.

Other than the dispatcher, Millie would need to man the office until she got back. Hopefully, there wouldn't be another crisis before the other swing shift deputy came in for duty.

Rafe and she went out to the cruiser, and Bree had to do something she rarely did. Glance around for a potential threat. A threat that could be right here on Main Street in front of the police station. But she did plenty of glancing today. So did Rafe, and that let her know he was on alert as much as she was.

"If it's not Tessa's remains, then whose are they?" Rafe asked her the moment they were in the cruiser. "Any ideas?"

That was the million-dollar question, and Bree didn't have an answer. "There haven't been any unsolved missing person cases since Tessa. And she wasn't technically a missing person because of those texts she sent to Wade and you. I mean, he filed a report, and my father and the deputies looked for her, but after a while, the search ended, and everyone assumed she'd gotten on with her life elsewhere."

"Yeah, I thought the same thing." Rafe paused. "Wade pulled out all the stops looking for her, and for months, he called me nearly every day, hoping I'd heard from her."

"But you didn't, right?" she pressed.

Rafe was quick to shake his head. "No. Nothing other

than that one text, and it came from her number. So, if she didn't personally send it, someone else used her phone to message me."

Bree considered that as she drove. "Did the text sound like something Tessa would send?"

"It did. She even ended with her usual kiss, kiss. Well, that was usual for the texts she sent to me," he added when Bree lifted her eyebrow.

She hadn't recalled Tessa ever putting that in a text to her, but then, that was something Tessa likely reserved for her lover.

And Bree had to shove that aside.

Fast.

No way did she want that in her head. The mental images of Rafe and Tessa naked and rolling around in bed. Then again, there were other things she didn't want in her head when it came to Rafe. Too bad those things—like this heat and attraction for him—didn't seem to want to be pushed away. That didn't matter though.

She wouldn't act on it.

She hoped.

Normally, it was easy to avoid Rafe since he didn't come into town that often. In fact, before she'd driven up and spotted him at the grave, Bree hadn't seen him in nearly two years. That'd been at a party for a mutual friend, and she had made the serious mistake of dancing with Rafe. Body to body. Heat to heat.

Yes, a big mistake.

Before that, she had only vague thoughts as to how it would feel to be in his arms. But with that long, slow dance, she'd gotten a taste of the man she had lusted after for as long as she had felt such things.

Thankfully, she didn't have time to dwell on that memory because she pulled to a stop in front of the entrance to Ollie's office. Just seeing the sign, Morgue, was extremely effective in aligning her thoughts to where they should be.

They stepped inside and immediately entered a small reception area. Unmanned at the moment, probably because the woman who usually worked here, Cicily Mendoza, was married to Deputy Carson Mendoza, and she was no doubt with him since he would be staying the night in the hospital.

"Back here," Ollie called out.

He'd obviously heard them come in, and he stuck his head around the door behind the reception desk. Motioning for them to follow him, Ollie led them into the autopsy room.

Bree had been here a couple of times, on those rare occasions when Ollie had wanted to give her a post-mortem report in person. Before today, only one of those visits had been because of a murder. A domestic dispute that had gone very wrong, and a man had been stabbed to death. However, the body that was beneath the sheet on a metal table would likely turn out to be murder victim number two.

"I've been working on her," Ollie said as he followed her gaze. "Her fingerprints have already been sent to the database so we might have an ID on her soon."

Good. Even though the worst had already happened to this woman, she'd died or been killed, Bree hated that she didn't have a name. Right now, she was just the body in the morgue.

"Did either of you take anything for the big assed bruises that I know you have?" Ollie asked, leading them toward a small office.

"No," Rafe and she muttered in unison. Though if Rafe felt the way she did, they should have.

Ollie sighed and pulled out a bottle of ibuprofen from his desk. He handed it to Bree and filled a cup of water from the small cooler in the corner. Both Rafe and she downed a couple of pills and thanked Ollie.

"Those are the photos," Ollie announced, pointing to the wall.

Bree had expected the CSI pictures to be on his desktop computer, but they were on the large screens. It reminded her of the way a doctor would review X-rays.

"I have a program to measure the bones from the images," Ollie went on while Rafe and she studied the three photos.

All gruesome, all reminders that once this had been a living, breathing person. And then there was the red jacket. Clearly visible in all the shots, and she could see that the skeletal arms were actually still inside the sleeves.

"I fed all the photos into the program," Ollie explained, and now he did turn his desktop screen for them to see. "I used the three dozen that the CSIs took because sometimes camera angles can distort size. In fact, that could have happened on these. You need to know that. This could be a wild goose speculation."

"Speculate," Bree insisted.

Ollie didn't waste any time doing that. "Tessa was five four. That's right, isn't it?" he asked Rafe.

Rafe nodded. He wasn't showing a lot of emotion in either his response or the way he was looking at the images of the bones. But this had to feel like a punch to the gut for him. Even if it wasn't Tessa, it was still someone.

And she was dead.

"Well, I believe this woman is two inches taller than Tessa," Ollie said.

Bree whipped her gaze back to the remains, but it was impossible for her to determine height just by eyeballing them. "But if she's not Tessa, then why is she wearing that jacket?"

Ollie pointed his index finger in a you-got-it gesture. "Ah, that's the mystery, isn't it? It could be another coat, though that doesn't seem likely." He zoomed in on the embroidered cuffs. "That's the same as Tessa's, right?" Again, Ollie looked at Rafe for confirmation.

"It is. Tessa had it custom-made from a shop in San Antonio." He dragged in a breath. "But it's possible the shop liked the design so much they made others. But what

51

are the odds that someone would buy that exact design and end up buried here in Tessa's hometown?"

Bree was going with a nil on this. "Too much of a coincidence."

"I agree," Rafe was quick to say. "And that leaves us with the possibility that the woman's killer put Tessa's jacket on her. Or that the woman is actually Tessa, and the measurements are off."

Bree didn't know which to hope for. Either those bones belonged to her childhood friend, or that friend was somehow connected to the murder of this woman wearing the jacket.

"What about the second body?" Rafe muttered, going back into the prep room. "Is it possible that's Tessa?"

Sweet heaven. Bree hadn't even considered it, but she was right on Rafe's heels when he went to have a look. However, what she saw had her stomach lurching. Because most of the woman's face had been obliterated. Clearly, she was not cut out to be a medical examiner.

"Yeah," Ollie said when Bree made a soft groan. He, too, had come into the prep room with them. "Not much left of her features to ID her. But yes, she would be the right height for Tessa. From my cursory exam, she has no birthmarks, no moles or scars." He shifted to Rafe. "Does that fit with Tessa?"

Rafe wasn't so quick to answer this time, and Bree figured he was pulling up some memories of Tessa when they'd been naked together. But Bree had her own memories that she could tap into.

"Tessa and I used to change together for swim class," she volunteered. "And I don't recall any kinds of blemishes on her skin. She was perfect."

Rafe nodded, maybe agreeing on both counts of the no blemishes and the perfection. And Bree got smacked with the past. With that old feeling that she would never be perfect like Tessa, that she would never be good enough for Rafe to take notice of her.

But he was noticing her now.

Bree looked at him and saw he was staring at her. No, he was studying her. For what? To see if this was bothering her?

Well, of course, it was.

But it was bothering her on two levels, both professional and personal, and the personal had to take a hike. She really didn't want to deal with old feelings of inadequacy and sexual frustration over her friend's guy.

"Tessa's prints aren't in the system," Ollie said, breaking the silence that had settled between them. "No criminal records. But if Wade has her prints somewhere, perhaps on some old item of hers, then maybe you can get those for a comparison."

Bree was already taking out her phone to text Wade, though she wished she could tap someone else for this. Wade was no doubt going through hell and back right now, and a request for his daughter's prints weren't going to make things easier. Still, it had to be done.

Within seconds after she sent the text, she got a response. "Wade kept all of Tessa's things," she let Ollie and Rafe know.

Since she didn't have an available deputy, she messaged Wade back to let him know she'd be at his house soon to gather the prints. Even if Wade was still at the hospital, he had a housekeeper who could let her in. She showed her text to Rafe so he'd know they needed to do that before returning to the station.

"Thanks for this," Bree told Ollie, and she tipped her head to the body. "And for the info about the bones. If you manage to get a more accurate time or cause of death, let me know."

Ollie assured her that he would, and Rafe and she headed out. As she'd done outside the police station, she had a cautious look around. There on Main Street, she hadn't seen anyone or anything out of the ordinary.

But she did now.

There was a black-haired man astride a motorcycle. He looked dangerous with his dark eyes, stony expression, and desperado stubble that seemed to go well past the fashionable stage. He pinned his attention to Rafe and her.

Bree automatically reached for her gun.

Rafe's response seemed to be automatic as well. He reached for her hand, taking it before she could draw her weapon. Her nerves were already firing hard and fast because of this lethal-looking man, but Rafe's touch—yes, that mere touch—fired her up even more.

Delores Fossen

"It's okay," Rafe said. "That's Jericho McKenna."

Jericho. The hotshot investigator on the Maverick Ops team. That took her off alert, and her nerves settled a little when the corner of Jericho's mouth lifted in a cocky smile. That softened some of those hard features and made her understand why some of the media coverage about him and the cold cases he'd solved had also mentioned his looks.

The man was certainly, well, hot.

He was so not her type though. She didn't go for the hotshot, bad-boy vibe. Her type was much more the man who'd sent her nerves zinging simply because he'd touched her hand. The quiet, dedicated protector. The good guy. The guardian angel. Maybe it was her unlucky fate that Rafe seemed to have her hormonal number.

"Don't you ever sleep?" Jericho asked Rafe as he climbed off the motorcycle.

"I got a couple of hours," Rafe said. "You?"

"None. I haven't even gotten home yet. Made the mistake of going to see a friend, and while she was fixing me a very late lunch, a tasking came in from Ruby." Jericho shifted his attention to her. "And I take it you're Bree, the sheriff. I'm Jericho," he said, extending his hand.

She shook it, felt the hard strength there. But it didn't give her body even a smidge of a tingle.

Yeah, Rafe held the reins when it came to her lustful urges.

"Rafe and I just came off a three-week shitshow assignment in Mexico that had plenty of its FUBAR moments," Jericho explained. "But we pulled it off. Saved the billionaire's kidnapped wife and brought her back home to her humble abode and her husband's loving arms."

So, a success. An apparently exhausting one. "The wife was part of that eighty percent," she muttered.

"Eighty?" Jericho questioned, but then he waved that off. "Ah, Rafe's stats, of course. Mine are slightly lower which is why Rafe is Ruby's go-to man whenever someone needs saving. This wife, well, she definitely needed saving." He didn't add more, and Bree didn't ask. "Heard you two nearly got blown up."

"Nearly," Rafe confirmed. "That's why I asked Ruby to check into anyone who has bomb-building skills who's connected to us, the construction site or any of the other players in this investigation."

She hadn't known Rafe had done that, but again, it was appreciated. Of course, she would do her own search as well.

Jericho whistled and shook his head. "That's a wide pool of possible suspects. Still, you gotta start somewhere." He added a shrug before he reached into his pocket for his phone. "Why don't we go inside so I can show you the tasking I got instead of a late lunch?"

As Rafe and she had done, he made a sweeping glance around them. While this part of the parking lot didn't have anyone coming and going, and there weren't any vehicles other than theirs and Ollie's, it wasn't a good idea for them to stand outside like this.

"This way," she said, and they went back into the morgue. "It's just us, Ollie," she called out. "We just need a quiet place to talk for a couple of minutes."

The ME stuck his head around the door, and she saw he was already suited up for the autopsy. He gave her a gloved thumbs up and disappeared back into the workroom.

"Interesting place for a chat," Jericho grumbled, but he seemed more amused than put off.

He held up his phone so they could see the photo on the screen. It was a grainy shot of two men, and she instantly recognized one of them.

"That's Gavin McCray." She moved in for a closer look. Definitely Gavin.

"It is," Jericho verified. "I used facial recognition on the database we have for camera feeds, and he popped up."

"Camera feeds?" she questioned.

"Traffic, store security, dashcams of cars, you name it," Jericho provided. "And, no, you probably can't use this specific photo if it needs to hold up in court, but I can give you the exact source so you can get your own copy."

She didn't care for shortcuts, but Bree focused on what Jericho had said. "*If it needs to hold up in court*?" she repeated. "Does that mean there's something illegal happening in this picture?"

"Probably." Jericho tapped the image of the other man. He was built like a bouncer and had a shaved head. "That's Buckner. His full name is Callum James Buckner, but he just goes by his surname. He's thirty-nine and lives in San Antonio. He's bad news. If you put together a profile of the worst asshole you wouldn't want to cross paths with, it'd be Buckner. A rich psychopath wannabe militia guy. He owns a nightclub that's probably a front for all sorts of illegal stuff."

"How does he know Gavin?" Rafe asked.

"Good question, and that falls into the TBL category. To be learned," Jericho explained to Bree. "This particular photo was captured three days ago in the parking lot of the construction company where Gavin works. I've got the actual feed, and I'll send it to you, but it looks to me as if this is a surprise visit from Buckner, that the two men didn't actually know each other before this."

"I don't suppose, by some miracle, we have audio on the feed?" Bree pressed.

Jericho shook his head. "But as we speak, Ruby is sending it through a lip-reading program, so she might come up with something. As it stands now though, there appears to be some kind of deal going on." He pulled up another photo of Buckner handing Gavin an envelope.

It was impossible to tell, but Bree was guessing there was cash inside. "Some kind of payoff," she muttered, and she quickly tried to put the pieces of this together. "I need to find out when the work crews got the assignment for the job at the inn."

"Three days ago," Jericho provided. He smiled again. "Hey, Ruby's good and fast. In fact, she determined that

Gavin got the assignment about an hour before this encounter with Buckner."

Bree gave that some thought. "So, Buckner could have known there was a body buried there, and he wanted Gavin to alert him if he uncovered it," she said, but then stopped and she shook her head. "Gavin doesn't look spooked enough in the photo for that."

"Bingo," Jericho said, and judging from Rafe's and his expressions, they'd already reached a slightly different conclusion. "Gavin is in debt up to his proverbial eyeballs, so I think Buckner approached him with a deal. Maybe a story about buried treasure or some other shit, and if Gavin finds it, he's to call Buckner right away."

Yes, that would make more sense. "And Buckner couldn't have just said, *Don't dig in this specific spot* because then that would have alerted Gavin. He has no criminal record, and he would understand that finding a body would pull him into a potential murder investigation."

"Bingo," Jericho repeated. "So, our boy Gavin takes the money, agrees to call if treasure is found. Instead, he finds some bones."

"Did he call Buckner?" Rafe asked.

"He did," Jericho confirmed and then looked at her. "Sorry, that's not admissible in court either, but when you search Gavin's phone records, you'll see he made a short call to an unregistered number. A burner. Ruby hasn't been able to confirm Buckner owns the burner, but Gavin might fess up once you hit him with the picture of Buckner and him together."

Bree took out her phone and tried to call Gavin again to get him in for questioning. Again, the call went to voicemail, causing her to curse.

"Gavin could have done a runner," she muttered, and she called a contact at SAPD, Detective Jace Malley, and she requested he send some officers out to Gavin's residence to check. If Gavin was gone, she'd need to do an APB.

Part of her wanted to curse at maybe letting Gavin get away. But this could be the break they needed. And she could thank Ruby and her Maverick Ops team for it. That eased some of the frustrations and doubt about having to investigate with civilian consultants and their corner cutting strategies.

Some.

But there was too much cop in her blood to want this to be anything more than a one off. Once she had a fully recovered team of deputies, then she'd be glad to see Rafe go.

Except she wouldn't.

And that caused Bree to do some more mental cursing. This thing she had for him was a distraction she couldn't afford right now. Thankfully, Jericho got her back on track by pulling up something else on his phone. Not a photo this time but rather a list of names.

"You'll get a copy of this, too," Jericho went on. "These are missing women who could possibly fit Tessa's description and the somewhat limited details we have of the woman that I suspect is on the autopsy table right now."

"I've seen the body, and I don't have a great description of her either," Rafe admitted. "Blonde hair. Not quite five and a half feet tall. A willowy build. No distinguishing marks, as we just learned." He paused. "Most of her face is missing so I can't tell you the color of her eyes."

Jericho cursed under his breath. "Well, the list has been sorted by height and coloring so that might help you narrow it down. Also, there are actually two lists. One is for women who've gone missing in the past thirty-six hours. That could cover the body you found. As for the bones, there's another group of women who've been missing more than a decade."

"Are any of the names specifically linked to Tessa, Canyon Ridge, the inn or Buckner?" Rafe asked.

"Not so far, but if there's a link, Ruby or you will find it." Jericho yawned, and he used his phone to send them the files they'd just been discussing. "As for me, I'm getting that lunch, some sleep, and then I'll give you what help I can." He looked at Bree. "You want that help by the book or with blurred lines?"

She sighed. "By the book."

Jericho sighed, too. "I have a healthy respect for the badge, for the law, but after some of the situations I've been in, I don't mistake the law for justice. Sometimes, they aren't close to being the same thing." He held up his hands in a mock surrender gesture. "But, hey, for you, I'll stay above board." He stopped, volleyed glances at both of them. "Are you two...together?"

She felt herself blush. Actually, blush. And she got the feeling Jericho had nearly used the f-word instead of *together*.

"No," Bree said, with Rafe following quickly with his own, "No. But we were blood friends," he added.

Jericho grinned. "You know that sounds creepy so I won't ask for details."

With that, Jericho muttered a goodbye and headed out, and once the roar of his motorcycle faded, that left Rafe and her there in the silence of the morgue. They'd gotten a mountain of information in this conversation, and they would no doubt get even more once they were back in the office. First though, she needed to get Tessa's prints, and she would have left to do just that if her phone hadn't rung.

"Detective Malley," she relayed to Rafe. "He's the SAPD cop I asked to have someone check on Gavin."

Maybe the cops had done that right away, but Bree got a bad feeling about this.

And the bad feeling was right.

"Sheriff O'Neil," Malley said once she'd answered. "I just got a report on the man you've been looking for. Gavin McCray. Sorry to inform you, but someone just found his body. He's dead."

Chapter Five

———— ☆ ————

While Bree drove toward Wade's, Rafe read the preliminary report he'd just gotten from Ruby. Detective Malley would be sending Bree one as well, an official one, but that would likely take hours. Rafe didn't see waiting that long when it wasn't illegal for Ruby to access the info she had.

"About forty-five minutes ago, Gavin's wife, Patricia, called 911, saying she'd come home from doing groceries and found him bleeding and unresponsive in the kitchen," Rafe read aloud. "EMTs responded, and Gavin was pronounced dead on the scene with a single gunshot wound to the side of the head." He checked the timeline. "He was already dead before you asked the detective to send out officers to check on him."

Rafe had added that because he knew Bree was mentally beating herself up right now. She was no doubt second-guessing what she should have done.

"This isn't your fault," Rafe spelled out when he saw how tight her grip was on the steering wheel.

"Maybe," she muttered, not sounding at all convinced of that. "Gavin had kids. Please tell me they weren't there when his wife found him."

At least Rafe could give her this. "No. The wife was alone, so I'm guessing the kids were at school or daycare."

Hell, he hoped so anyway. Rafe hoped the children

hadn't been in the house. But even if they were, they clearly hadn't been harmed or Ruby would have put that in her report.

"I should have taken Gavin into custody after the explosion," she grumbled. "Instead, I let him wander off from the hospital, and look where that got him. Dead." She paused only a heartbeat. "I'm liking Buckner for this. You?"

"Oh, yeah. And Ruby agrees. She included Buckner's home address, business address, and contact info for phones at both of those places, along with his personal cell. She figured you'd be wanting to have a word with him."

"Definitely. A word where he tells me why the hell he's doing all this." She relaxed the grip on the steering wheel so she could slap it with her palm.

It didn't surprise him that something like this would eat away at Bree. Her blood ran blue, a legacy that went with being a fourth-generation cop. Even as a kid, she'd had a strong sense of right, wrong, and injustice.

"Pull over," Rafe said, pointing to the small parking area outside the massive wrought iron gates that fronted Wade's estate.

"It's not going to do any good to talk about it," she insisted.

"Pull over," he repeated.

He was thankful when she actually did it. Since they'd learned on the drive that Wade was home, Bree needed a minute to settle before she faced him. Wade was likely to be dealing with his own emotional mess, and Bree needed to have all her resolve gathered to handle him.

"Remember when we were eight, and you tripped Bodie Betterton in the hall at school?" He didn't wait for her to confirm the memory. Rafe knew that was something she'd never forget. "He'd gotten pissed at me about something and jumped me from behind in the locker room at gym class. Because he was twice my size, he beat me to a pulp before the coach got him off me."

"And while you were in the nurse's office, I saw Bodie and stuck out my foot to trip him," she finished. "I was so pissed off at him for hurting you that I wanted to hurt him right back."

"You did just that." Rafe chuckled. "Bodie faceplanted on very hard, very dirty linoleum that I'm convinced was bulletproof. He broke his nose and had to walk around school with one of those ugly face braces for weeks."

Bree didn't laugh. But she did smile a little. "I lied and said it was an accident, and all the eyewitnesses backed me up because Bodie was an asswipe bully." She stopped, put the cruiser into park, and turned to look at him. "Is there a life lesson in that?"

"Several of them. First, always trip the asswipe bully if you can. Maybe not with a literal trip, but asswipes should have to pay for what they'd done."

She gave him a flat look and tapped her badge as if to tell him that it was never a good idea to take the law into one's own hands. Or in her case, one's own foot.

"And the second life lesson is that sometimes even

when we do the right thing, it might not feel right," he spelled out. "Even now, you feel guilty for what you did to Bodie. Am I right?"

She cut her gaze away from him. Yeah, she felt guilty all right. Rafe not so much, but then he'd been on the receiving end of the pounding from Bodie.

"If I'd at least questioned Gavin, then we might have had some proof that Buckner is behind this," she muttered.

Rafe didn't point out that she had been partly in shock from the explosion, that she'd had a dozen other investigative balls in the air. And at that time, they hadn't known for certain that Gavin would turn out to be a key player. Because pointing all that out wouldn't do anything to relieve what she was feeling.

Hell, what he was feeling, too.

He knew they'd missed their chance to learn something important. That bridge was burned now though, and they just had to find other info that would make sense of this situation. What wouldn't make sense was what Rafe felt himself doing, and what he was doing was unhooking his seatbelt.

And pulling Bree into his arms.

Oh, yeah. Big mistake.

That didn't stop him though. He just pulled her to him, drawing her closer and closer until there was some contact with their upper bodies.

Good contact.

The kind that notched up this heat he'd been feeling

for her since that dance two years ago. Even before that, Rafe had always felt the attraction. Of course, he'd kept that stomped down for a very long time because of Tessa. Because they were all friends. But it seemed like too much to try to stomp right now.

Much to his surprise, Bree didn't jolt away from him and tell him how inappropriate this was. Just the opposite. She stayed there in his arms, not stiff and defensive either. She sort of melted against him.

Oh, this was trouble.

No doubt about it. He already had the potential loss of focus, what with Tessa's body maybe being found, but it was double dangerous to add this heat to the mix. Still, he stayed there, doing his own melting, until they finally eased back from each other.

"Sorry," she muttered. "That shouldn't have happened."

Rafe sighed and wanted to curse. He didn't get a chance to do either because his phone dinged with a text.

"It's from Wade," he relayed. "The gate alerted him that we were out here, and he sent me the security code."

Rafe glanced at the gate and then at the discrete metal box next to it. And he saw the tiny camera.

Well, shit.

If Wade had witnessed that hug, he might have questions. Then again, there were plenty more important things to discuss than Bree and him in an embrace.

The text seemed to snap Bree back to cop mode, and

she drove up to the box. Rafe rattled off the code, she punched it in, and the gates immediately started to open. They drove through onto a pristine private road lined with stately oak trees. All very impressive. As was the house.

Correction, the mansion.

The three-story Georgian sprawled across the landscape like some English manor. Which had been Wade's intentions. His mother had been born in England in such a house, and he'd wanted to recreate it. He'd succeeded and clearly poured a lot of money not only into the mansion itself but into the gardens.

Bree pulled to a stop in the circular drive, but as they were getting out, Rafe's phone dinged again. "From Ruby," he told Bree as they made their way toward the front door. "The forensic anthropologist now has the recovered bones and will expedite getting the DNA from them."

"How soon will we have results?" Bree asked.

"Probably not until morning. The anthropologist can't use what's called Rapid DNA,which would give results in a couple of hours because she has to extract the DNA from the bones. But once she has the DNA, she can compare it to Wade's, which will in turn prove if it's Tessa."

Bree didn't have a chance to react to that because Wade threw open the double doors. "I need an update," he blurted right off. It was obvious these past couple of hours had been hell on the man. "Please. Just tell me anything you know."

Bree nodded, and Wade moved out of the doorway so

they could go inside to the foyer—which was larger than most living rooms.

Rafe knew this wasn't Bree's first visit here to the estate. She'd come here often with Tessa, but like Rafe, she still glanced around the way one might if they'd just stepped into a museum or art gallery. Like the yard and the tree-lined drive, Wade hadn't spared any expense inside the house either.

"I can fill you in while I try to get the fingerprints," Bree explained.

"Right. Yes, that," Wade said as if he'd forgotten all about the reason for the visit. "This way. Like I said, I left nearly everything in her room as is. I didn't want things changed too much for when she came back. If she came back," he added under his breath.

Even though there was an impressive staircase at the end of the foyer, Wade led them toward the elevator tucked into an alcove at the side of the stairs. This was a new addition, Rafe noticed, maybe because Wade had grown tired of going up three flights to reach the top floor where he had his bedroom suite.

Tessa's room was on that floor as well, and while Rafe had been to the house plenty of times, he'd only made it to Tessa's bedroom once. And that'd been under the careful eye of a housekeeper while Tessa grabbed her purse as they were leaving on a date. Wade's rules were that Tessa wasn't allowed to have boys there.

"Go back to the time Tessa disappeared," Bree

instructed Wade as they exited the elevator on the third floor. "Why do you think she left?"

Wade's breath was weary, and it matched his expression to a tee. "I've gone over that a thousand times or more."

"I know. But please go over it again," she coaxed. "Sometimes, by repeating it, you remember a little thing that could be important."

Wade stopped outside Tessa's suite. "Why? Have you found something?" But he waved that off and opened the door to let them into the room. "Get the prints and I'll talk about Tessa."

But Wade didn't jump into the subject of his daughter. He stepped inside the room. And just stood there. No doubt dealing with all the memories of seeing her things.

Like the rest of the house, sprawling was the right word for this room, too, with sitting and desk areas along with the king-sized bed. Since the door was open to the ensuite bath, Rafe could see it matched the large scale of the rest of the room.

Bree had a sweeping glance around and headed to a lighted vanity table just inside the bathroom. Wade had been right about keeping things as is. The vanity was jammed with cosmetics and hair stuff.

"Tessa had been in a bad mood for weeks before she left," Wade finally started while Bree gloved up and took the fingerprint kit from her bag. "Heck, she'd been in a bad mood since her mother died a few months earlier from breast cancer."

Rafe knew that was true. Tessa and her mother hadn't been close. Just the opposite. They'd been more oil and water than mother and daughter. Lots of arguments and sometimes months of sullenness where they never even spoke to each other. When her mom had died, Rafe thought that Tessa felt guilty that she hadn't at least been more caring during those last days.

"Tessa was riled, too, because she didn't want you to leave and refused the notion of following you around the world on assignments," Wade added to Rafe.

Good thing, too, since there wouldn't have been much following him around. Combat Rescue Officers spent a lot of time on deployments where their families couldn't go.

"But I'm not saying she left because of you," Wade insisted. "It was more than that. She was moody and restless. She was staying out all night. And, yeah, I know that's something a girl her age does. *A woman*," he corrected in a mutter. "But she was secretive about who she was seeing and what she was doing."

"I have to ask," Bree said as she dusted the handle of a hairbrush for the prints. "Do you think she was using drugs?"

"No," Wade insisted. Then, he paused. "But she came in hungover a couple of times. I just don't think she had direction in her life. She didn't know what to do with herself."

That meshed with what Rafe believed, too. Tessa had never pressed him for marriage, and she'd never done especially well in college. In fact, she'd flunked out. With no desire to help run her father's business, Tessa had basically shopped and partied.

Rafe took out his phone and pulled up Buckner's photo. "Did you ever see Tessa with this man?"

Wade took the phone, adjusting his glasses for a long look before he shook his head. "No. I know she never brought him here. Why? Is he a suspect?"

"A person of interest," Bree supplied while she continued with the prints. "And, no, I'm not giving you his name because I don't want you to contact him. Right now, I just need to talk to him."

"But he might have killed my baby girl," Wade muttered.

Bree finished with the prints, using the app on her phone to start processing them, and she came back into the bedroom, stopping right in front of Wade. "I'm begging you not to get up your hopes about what I'm going to tell you. Just understand that it's speculation at this point."

"What?" Wade's gaze was now pinned to Bree's.

"Ollie examined photos of the bones, and he thinks there's a possibility that they don't belong to Tessa."

"What?" Wade repeated, but this time it wasn't a demand. It was filled with anxious breath. And hope. No way for a father not to hang onto that.

"A possibility," Bree emphasized. "That's why the DNA is important. Thanks to Ruby Maverick and her team, we might have a DNA profile tomorrow on the bones taken from the grave. Then, we'll know for sure."

Wade stayed quiet a moment, obviously considering that, and even though it was a *possibility*, it caused him to grope around behind him for the bed. He sank down onto the mattress as if his legs had given out on him.

"DNA," Wade repeated. "Won't they need to match Tessa's DNA to the bones?"

"They will," Rafe spoke up, and he knew it was time for him to confess what he'd done. "The blood on your handkerchief will be used to build a DNA profile for Tessa."

Wade blinked and shook his head as if confused. "My blood," he said, and that seemed to yank him back to the moment. "Yes, that makes sense." He stopped though, and the confusion returned. "If you have my blood, then why are you here for fingerprints?" Wade asked after several moments. "Have you got something to match them to?" His eyes widened, and his breath appeared to vanish. "The other dead woman. The one that Davy spotted with his binoculars. Is that Tessa?"

"We don't know," Bree answered.

That got Wade back on his feet. "I can try to ID the body."

She took hold of his arm when he headed for the door. "No. There's too much damage from the explosion for that."

"Bree's right," Rafe added. "We both saw the body, and we can't say for sure."

Again, Wade went quiet. "Then, maybe neither of them is Tessa. My baby girl could still be alive."

"It's possible," Bree said, but she didn't sound convinced.

Rafe agreed with her. It'd been eighteen years, plenty of time for Tessa to have resurfaced. So, either she was dead or didn't want to be found. He just wished he knew which it was.

"Should I call someone to stay with you?" Rafe asked Wade.

Wade shook his head. "Just run those prints and get those DNA results. I'm not going to rest easy until I have those."

He stopped, sighed, and Rafe knew that even with the results, Wade wouldn't be getting much rest. Not until he knew the truth about his daughter. And then, depending on what he learned, he would likely begin a full-scale search to find Tessa.

Or start grieving her death.

Bree gave Wade's shoulder a gentle squeeze. "I'll let you know as soon as I hear anything."

Since Wade didn't stand, Rafe and Bree showed themselves out. They'd barely made it out of the elevator when her phone rang.

"It's Millie," she said, referring to Deputy Millie Hernadez. "You're on speaker," Bree let her know. "And Rafe is here with me."

Rafe hoped Millie wouldn't hold back anything just

because he was listening, but the deputy didn't even hesitate. "I just got an updated list of names of missing women who might match the body Ollie has in the morgue. Rafe's boss sent it over and said she'd forwarded a copy to Ollie."

Updated. That meant either Ruby had refined it or had found even more possible candidates.

"Did anyone on the list jump out at you?" Bree asked her.

"No. I didn't recognize a single name. But the list includes photos and details like distinguishing marks, so maybe Ollie will be able to make a match."

"Maybe," Bree said, not sounding very hopeful. Probably because she'd remembered that much of the woman's face had been obliterated. "I just gathered Tessa's prints and sent them for processing. We might get a hit." When they reached the front door, they went back outside to the cruiser. "How are things going there?"

"Surprisingly quiet. I put out the word we didn't have time to deal with gossips and to only come into the station if they had something solid to contribute to the investigation."

"Good. And have you gotten any updates on Alice and Carson?" Bree asked.

"Yes. Carson called to say that Alice is staying overnight in the hospital. He's being released but has to stay on bed rest for at least twenty-four hours. Say, why aren't you on bed rest?" Millie tacked onto that.

"Because I don't need it. I'm fine."

Millie made a sound to indicate she didn't quite buy that. Neither did Rafe. Bree should be taking at least a couple of hours of downtime to level out and process that attack. But he couldn't call her on it since he wasn't leveling or processing either.

"We'll be back at the station in about ten minutes," Bree said to Millie as she ended the call. She didn't say anything else until they'd made it through the gates. "You think you should call someone for Wade?"

"Honestly, I wouldn't know who to call. He doesn't have family, and I'm not privy to his friends. If you think it should happen though, I could get Ruby to get me the contact info."

She stayed quiet a moment, then shook her head. "I don't think Wade would harm himself. Not at this point anyway. But if there's bad news, and either the body or the bones turn out to be Tessa's, then he'll need someone."

Yeah, he would. Rafe figured Wade had gone through hell when Tessa had disappeared. The not knowing must have eaten away at him. But facing his child's death would be a whole new level of misery and grief.

Bree's phone rang again, and he saw San Antonio PD flash on the dash monitor. She answered it right away, using the handsfree, and after she identified herself, she informed the caller about being on speaker and that a consultant was listening.

"This is Jace Malley," the man said, and Rafe recalled

this was the detective who'd informed her about Gavin's death. "I thought you'd want to know there was a suicide note found alongside Gavin's body in the kitchen of his home."

Bree sighed. "What did it say?"

"I'll read it verbatim. *I'm so sorry. I'm a coward. I killed those two women found at the old inn, and I can't face what I've done. I love you, and tell the kids I love them, too. Please try to forgive me.*"

"Is it in his handwriting?" Bree quickly asked, voicing the question that was first and foremost in Rafe's mind.

"The wife says it is," the detective confirmed. "She'll be questioned, of course, but for now, she's saying she had no idea that anything was wrong, that he hasn't been acting strange. No marital problems, according to her, and that he was a loving, devoted husband and father." He paused. "You think Gavin could have been coerced into ending his own life?"

"It's possible," she muttered.

"If he had written the note of his own free will, he likely would have mentioned the wife and kids by name," Rafe spoke up. "He would have probably tried to give an explanation for what he was doing."

"True," Bree added. "We don't have identities on either body, but when I have them, we can search for any connections between Gavin and them. And if there are indeed connections, we'll need to find out why he dumped the bodies here in Canyon Ridge."

That led Rafe to another of his concerns. "If Gavin did dump them, then why not try to conceal the bodies? He was operating the excavator so he could have shifted enough dirt to cover the first one, rather than expose it."

"I see your point," Jace agreed. "I'll do some digging on my end and see if I can come up with anything. He paused again. "You work for Ruby Maverick's team?" the detective asked.

"I do," Rafe verified.

"Maybe sometime we can get together, and I can pick your brain about what it's like to work for her. I'm thinking about trying to join Maverick Ops."

It wasn't a totally out of the blue remark. Plenty of cops, PIs, and former military wanted to join. It wasn't easy though to get in, and Ruby wasn't easily swayed by the people she wanted on, or off, the team.

"After this case, we can talk," Rafe assured him, and Bree ended the call.

"So, you're not buying that Gavin ended his own life," she immediately said. "Neither am I, and Buckner could have been the one to coerce him."

Bree gave the voice command to call Buckner at one of the numbers that she'd gotten from Ruby. First one. Then, two. Then, the third. All three went straight to voicemail, causing Bree to curse under her breath.

"I might have to pay him a visit in San Antonio," she said. "I don't want Malley to do that. I want to see and hear for myself what Buckner has to say."

Rafe agreed. But there was another factor here. "You have to be exhausted. Best to have a clear head when you talk to him."

She didn't argue with either part of that. "All right, first thing in the morning then. In the meantime, I'll continue to call until I either get him on one of the lines or he blocks me."

It seemed she was on the verge of repeating those calls right then, but her own phone rang. For one hopeful moment, Rafe thought it might be Buckner, but it wasn't any of his numbers that popped up.

"This is Teddy Sanchez," the caller said, his voice pouring through the cruiser when Bree answered. "I'm head of the county bomb squad. Just wanted to let you know that we've cleared the scene. We didn't find any other explosives, so it's safe if you want to come back out here and have a look around."

"I do," Bree verified, and she executed a U-turn using a ranch trail that threaded off the road. "I'll be there soon."

"Good," Sanchez said. "Because there's something here you'll definitely want to see."

Chapter Six

—————— ☆ ——————

Bree could feel the exhaustion in every muscle in her body. The post-adrenaline crash had drained her, which was why it was standard procedure for her police department to take at least twenty-four hours off after some high-risk encounter.

The explosion was definitely high risk, and she would indeed get that rest. Just not a full twenty-four hours. And not right now. She needed to see what Teddy Sanchez, the bomb squad expert, wanted to show her.

She pulled her cruiser to a stop behind the row of vehicles that were parked in front of the inn. The bomb squad SUV, the CSIs' van, and the fire marshal's truck. Bree hadn't expected to see Davy back here, but then he would no doubt want to learn Sanchez's findings as well.

After Bree texted Millie to let the deputy know about the change in plans, Rafe and she got out of the cruiser and made a beeline toward Davy, who was next to a lanky dark-haired man that she figured must be Sanchez. She hadn't had cause to meet him before now, so she made introductions as they approached.

"I'm Sheriff Bree O'Neil," she said, "and this is Rafe Cross, consultant."

Even though the consultant label was true, saying it still didn't feel natural coming out of her mouth. Then again, it didn't feel natural to have one involved in her investigation either.

"Teddy Sanchez," the man greeted in return. "Good to meet you, and thanks for coming. I'll put everything I'm about to go over with you in my report, but like I said, I figured you'd want to see it for yourself."

Bree made a sound of agreement and glanced around. She tried not to have any flashbacks of nearly being killed here. Hard to do though with the fatigue and the nightmarish images flashing through her head. Still, she made herself focus since revisiting the scene could help with the investigation.

Clearly, others had the same idea.

Two CSIs were still photographing and combing the grounds. A young man in a bomb squad uniform was near the spot where the bones had been found. Next to him was one of Davy's firemen.

Sanchez pointed to the spot where the CSIs were. "That's the point of origin for the blast," he explained. "As you can see, it's a good ten yards from the grave you found." He shifted, pointing toward a spot further up the private road from where they were all parked. "It looks as if whoever dumped the body and set the device came from that direction."

"Are there footprints or tire tracks?" she immediately asked.

"Nothing identifiable," Sanchez informed her. "Just some trampled down weeds. No drag marks, though, so it's my conclusion that both the body and the device were carried to their respective sites." He turned again and pointed to what was left of a stone cottage that had probably once been occupied by a groundskeeper. "The device to detonate the explosives was likely in there."

"No footprints leading there either," Davy was quick to add. "Just more trampled down weeds and broken twigs."

"Nothing inside either," Sanchez said, taking up the explanation, "but there's a small cleared-out area in the dust and dirt that makes me believe something was there. It's the right size to have been a detonator."

That gave Bree a fresh punch of the bad images. Of being knocked off her feet. The pain. The fear. Yes, there'd been some of that once she'd realized what was happening.

"Perhaps there was a timer on the detonator," Sanchez speculated. "If so, it could have been set when the body was dumped." He made a sound of frustration. "But it's equally possible someone had their hands on the detonator and didn't need a timer. If so, the person had to be in the area, likely in that cottage."

"Gavin was out of sight for a while," Rafe reminded her. "When you got to the scene and asked who'd found the body, I looked for Gavin, but he wasn't here."

Yes, and that meant Gavin could have indeed been setting the timer and making sure he was just far enough out of range not to be killed. But that still didn't answer why he'd done all of this.

Bree put that question on the back burner and glanced around at the spots Sanchez had pointed out. "How far was the explosive device from the woman's body that was found?"

"About ten yards," Sanchez quickly provided. "It'd been placed between the grave and her."

"So, the explosion was maybe meant to destroy both the body and the bones," Rafe muttered under his breath. "Along with anyone else close enough to it who was investigating the scene."

That's where Bree's thoughts had gone as well. "But why would someone want to do that?" she asked more to herself than to anyone else. "Why not just move the bodies where there was a smaller chance of them being discovered in the first place?"

"I have no idea," Sanchez said, and Davy echoed the same. It was Davy who continued.

"And I'm going to complicate things by relaying info I got from Gavin's boss at the construction company. Gavin wasn't supposed to be digging in that spot. He was supposed to be in the east garden." Davy pointed to an area just past some overgrown hedges. "He was supposed to be leveling that."

Bree shook her head and tried to figure out what that meant. "So, did he know the body was there? Is that why he was digging?"

"It's something you'll want to ask him, that's for sure," Davy concluded.

"We can't," Rafe spoke up. "He's dead."

"Dead?" Sanchez and Davy repeated in unison.

Bree nodded. "Either someone killed him and set it up to try to make it look like a suicide, or else he died by his own hand. I'm going with option one on this." Neither Sanchez nor Davy disagreed with her on that. "And I think whoever killed him did it because of this." She pointed to the grave site and where the body had been found.

"You believe he murdered Tessa and the other woman?" Davy asked.

"If it is Tessa," Bree said. "It's possibly someone else, and that's just the start of the questions I don't have answers for." She glanced around again. "The explosion feels like a way to destroy evidence and stall the investigation."

All four of them stayed quiet for several moments. "If Gavin killed those two women, he could have destroyed the evidence before the construction started," Rafe commented.

"He wouldn't have dug where he did, either" Sanchez added. "So, who killed all three?"

Another question for which she didn't have an answer. Yet. Bree took out her phone, pulled up Buckner's photo and showed them.

"Have either of you seen this man?" she asked.

Both studied it and then shook their heads. "Who is he?" Sanchez wanted to know.

"A person of interest," Bree provided. "I intend to find

out if he has any explosive's expertise."

Of course, according to Jericho's report, Buckner was rich so he would likely hire minions for that sort of thing. Still, he'd personally met with Gavin. They had proof of that with a photo, so maybe Buckner had done hands on with the explosive device as well.

Sanchez's phone rang, and he stepped aside to take the call. Bree was about to walk to the CSIs to talk to them, but Davy stopped her.

"Let me see Buckner's picture again," Davy said.

Surprised, she studied him as she brought it up. "You think you might know him?"

Davy shrugged, took her phone and zoomed in on the face. "I'm not sure. The bald head was throwing me off, but he sort of resembles some guy I saw with Tessa."

Rafe's head whipped up, and his gaze zoomed in on Davy. Bree didn't miss the look in his eyes. Not jealousy. At least she didn't think it was. Or maybe that was wishful thinking.

"Sort of resembles," Davy emphasized. He stopped, sighed. And cursed. "Look, it might be him." He scrubbed his hand over his face. "Please tell me you knew that Tessa was seeing other men after you went off to college."

"I knew," Rafe confirmed without hesitating even a second. "You think she saw Buckner?"

"Or someone who resembles him," Davy said, the frustration edging his voice. "Hell, Rafe. It's been nearly twenty years, and after you left, Tessa saw lots of men."

"Did she *see* you?" Bree asked.

Davy's hesitation said it all, but she waited for the verbal confirmation. "Once. Just once," he repeated, shifting back to Rafe. "And it wasn't planned or anything." He paused again and did more cursing. "Look, Tessa got into some dangerous shit. She'd go to bars, drink too much, and pick up strangers for sex. Did you know about that?" he asked, directing the question to Rafe.

"I heard some gossip. I never confronted Tessa about it because it was pretty clear to me then that we weren't going to stay a couple."

That seemed to level Davy out some. "All right." He repeated that several times. "Okay, so one night I was in a bar in San Antonio, and I saw her making out with this guy. He got rough with her, was pushing her around, and I stepped in. Long story short, I ended up getting her out of there. She didn't want to go home and face her dad, so we went to my place. And we had sex," he tacked onto that in a mutter.

"Was the man she was with possibly Buckner?" Rafe asked. Again, he didn't seem affected by all this personal garbage he was hearing about Tessa.

"No. I'm sure of that. Nothing about Buckner matches any of the description I remember about that guy in the bar. But I was at a party about six months later, and I saw her with a man who could have been Buckner. With hair," he emphasized. "He definitely wasn't bald and not quite so bulky looking as he is in the picture."

A person's appearance could change a lot in eighteen years, especially since Buckner would have only been in his early twenties back then.

"Six months later," Rafe muttered, taking out his phone. "How soon was this before Tessa disappeared?"

Davy's forehead bunched up. "Not long. Maybe a month or two." He shifted to Bree. "That could be in the statement that I gave your dad when he investigated Tessa leaving. I think I mentioned the last time I saw her was at a party and that she was with some guy. I might have even given a description of him."

Both Rafe and she got to work. Her, texting Millie to have her pull up those old files. Rafe was sending a text, too, probably to Ruby or someone else on his team. Maybe one of them would be able to find some proof that Buckner had indeed known Tessa. That way, it would free up Rafe and her to do the leg work, such as tracking down Buckner for an interview and possible arrest.

In her mind, he'd just moved up from person of interest to a solid suspect.

"I'm going to call Detective Malley at SAPD and ask him if they can do a check on Buckner," Bree said once Rafe had finished his text. "I don't want him to rabbit on us and fly off to some country where he can't be extradited."

She turned to say her goodbyes to Davy and Sanchez, who was still on the phone, but the sound of an engine stopped her. Bree looked up the road and saw the minivan speeding toward them.

Emphasis on speeding.

The driver was going way too fast, especially for such a narrow road, and it wasn't a vehicle Bree recognized. Still, there were a lot of investigators in and out of the scene, and for a moment, she considered it could be one of them.

But only for a moment.

The van crashed into the back of the cruiser, not wrecking either the van or the cruiser but hitting it hard enough to make a loud noise. It seemed in the same motion, a tall blonde woman bolted from the driver's side. She immediately lifted a handgun.

And fired at them.

The shot blasted through the air, and the woman ducked back behind the van, using it as cover while she sent another bullet their way.

Rafe took hold of Bree, pulling her to the ground, but she had already been heading in that direction anyway. She hit hard and felt the impact in every bruise she'd gotten from the explosion.

A third shot blasted into the ground just inches from Bree's head, and a fresh round of pain knifed through her. It took her a moment to realize she hadn't been hit by a bullet but rather a small rock that the bullet had kicked up. It'd slammed into her forehead.

"Move," Rafe ordered.

He didn't wait for her to comply though. He took hold of her again, initiating a combat-style crawl behind a large landscape boulder. Across from them, Davy and Sanchez did the same, taking cover behind Davy's truck.

She wasn't sure Davy was even armed, but Sanchez had drawn his gun. He wouldn't have a clean shot at their attacker though, not unless the woman came out from that van or if he moved out. Bree was hoping he wouldn't do that. She had no idea just how good of a shot this woman was, but Sanchez wasn't wearing any kind of protective gear to stop bullets.

None of them were.

Bree made a quick glance behind them and saw that the two CSIs, the second bomb expert, and the other fireman had all dropped down to the ground as well. The bomb guy, too, had pulled a gun, but his angle for a shot was even worse than Sanchez's. Their best bet right now would be just to stay down, especially since the bullets hadn't gone in their direction.

"You bitch," the woman yelled. And she fired another shot. This one hit the boulder and sent shards of the rock flying.

Since Bree was the only woman in the vicinity, that meant this attack was likely directed at her. Sweet heaven. But why? She didn't know the shooter.

Did she?

"Stay here," Rafe whispered. "I'm going to try to get behind her."

Bree had no idea how he could do that since they were pretty much out in the open except for the boulder. Once he left cover, he'd be an easy target.

Except he wasn't the target.

She was.

Still, if this woman was unstable, there was no telling who she might shoot to get to Bree. "Be careful," she added to Rafe as he got into a crouching position.

Then, he launched himself out into the open like a sprinter in a race, and he ran. Fast. And not in a straight line either. He was zigzagging toward the bomb squad van, which was the vehicle nearest them.

Bree held her breath, praying that he didn't get gunned down. The woman did fire a single shot at him, missing him, but then she turned the gun back in Bree's direction. Two more shots slammed into the boulder, and Bree heard the rock crack.

Mercy.

If the shots managed to take off enough chunks of it, she'd be a much easier target to kill. And it was obvious this woman wanted her dead.

"Who are you and what do you want?" Bree shouted.

She had a twofold reason for the questions. First, she wanted to distract the woman so she wouldn't shoot Rafe. That was top priority right now. But Bree also wanted answers to know what she was up against.

"I want you to die for killing my husband," the woman yelled back.

"Your husband?" Bree asked, and there was surprise in her voice because she had no idea what the woman was talking about. She'd never killed anyone, not even in the line of duty.

"My husband," she said, the last word trailing off into a sob. Bree could hear the woman crying now and muttering something Bree didn't catch. However, she did catch the next part. "Gavin is dead, and you killed him."

Gavin. So, this was his wife, Patricia.

"I didn't kill him," Bree insisted.

"You did," she shrieked. "I know you did. You made him write that note, and you murdered him. Now, you're going to die, too."

She fired more shots, enough that Bree thought she had probably emptied the clip. If she'd come for revenge though, she would have perhaps brought more ammunition.

"I didn't kill Gavin," Bree tried again. "But I believe someone did. I'm investigating it."

"You're covering up what you did," was her response.

There was no reason in her tone. She was hysterical, and in that moment, Bree knew there was nothing she could say to make Patricia understand that she hadn't murdered Gavin.

But someone had convinced her of that.

Someone persuasive enough to enrage her and turn her into a lethal weapon hellbent on revenge.

"Gavin would have never taken his own life," Patricia went on. "He loved me and our children." She broke down into another sob.

Bree saw the blur of motion on the woman's left. Just a

blur. Before Rafe rammed into the woman, tackling her and dragging her to the ground. In the same motion, he clamped his hand on her right wrist. On her shooting hand.

It was too late though to stop her from firing.

The final shot blasted from her gun.

Chapter Seven

———— ☆ ————

Rafe hoped like hell that he'd had his last adrenaline surge of the day. Even in his dangerous line of work, it was rare for him to face death twice in the span of less than twelve hours.

No doubt even rarer, or never, for Bree.

He could still hear the sound of those shots Patricia had fired at her. Especially the last one. The shot Rafe hadn't been able to stop before he'd tackled her. Patricia had managed to pull the trigger one last time, and that bullet had come damn close to Bree again.

Too close.

It had torn into the ground literally an inch from where she was. One inch over, and Bree would have had more than minor injuries and the memories from hell. She could have been dead.

Bree wasn't the only one who'd have hellish memories about that though.

No.

Rafe was going to have to fight those images if he hoped to keep even a sliver of objectivity. About the investigation. And especially about her.

Like him, she was exhausted from the adrenaline crash and the event of this long, shitty day, but it hadn't been her exhaustion that had allowed him to convince her to let him take her home. It'd been her uniform.

And the blood on it.

The stitches on her forehead had maybe played into the decision, too, to call it a day. Along with all her other bruises from the explosion, the pain from that particular injury had perhaps made her agree to put the pause button on the investigation with the plans to go home, eat, shower, and get some much-needed rest.

Rafe had accomplished the first two with them devouring some leftover lasagna from her fridge. The third—the shower—was in progress, and since he was sitting on the foot of her bed, he could hear the shower still running and knew she was taking her time in there. And probably being careful not to get her stitches wet. He was hoping that the hot water and the over-the-counter pain meds she'd already taken would help relax her enough so she could get some sleep. He'd need sleep, too, but he would also be keeping watch.

What he hadn't been able to do was convince her to go to his place, which had much better security. Still, she did live in a safe neighborhood on the outskirts of town, and she had a burglar alarm they'd already set, so that would have to do.

For now.

But precautions needed to be taken.

He was even more convinced of that as he read the last report Jericho had just sent him. Rafe was in the process of rereading it when he heard the shower stop, and several minutes later, Bree came out of the ensuite wearing loose pajamas with...dancing frogs on them.

"A gag gift from my Secret Santa," she muttered when she followed his confused gaze.

Her short hair was dry, which meant she'd definitely avoided getting those stitches wet, but the lower part of her face was still dotted with beads of water she'd obviously missed while drying off. She smelled like lavender soap.

And sex.

Okay, that last part was no doubt his overactive libido and the thoughts of his brainless dick. This night couldn't involve sex. Only sleep and as much comfort as he could give her. Still, he couldn't help noticing her long, bare legs and the way those ugly pajamas fit her curves.

"How's the head?" he asked.

She shrugged. "Minor stuff. But I have a bruise on my right butt cheek that looks like a giant Easter egg."

That made him smile, and there was indeed plenty to smile about. They were alive, and no one else at the scene of the shooting had been injured. With as many shots as Patricia had fired, that was somewhat of a miracle.

"What were you reading?" she asked, tipping her head to his phone. She didn't come closer, but she seemed to want to get him to focus on something else other than her.

It was possible—no, damn likely—that he was gawking at her. Possibly drooling, too. And there was no way he could take the heat out of his eyes. Well, not while he was looking at her, so he tore his attention from her and put it back on his phone.

"It's a report from Jericho," he said. "There have been no unusual deposits in Gavin's bank account, so the envelope Buckner gave him likely contained cash. No sign of Buckner either," he let her know since Rafe knew she would ask.

Now, it was his turn to nod toward the phone she had gripped in her hand. "What about you? I heard you get a couple of texts while you were in the bathroom."

She nodded. Sighed. "Updates on Patricia. She's been admitted to a county psychiatric hospital for evaluation. She can't be questioned until she's classified as stable, and I have no idea when that will be. If ever," she added in a mumble.

The worry and fatigue came, rushing over her and erasing some of the eased tension he'd seen in her right after she'd come into the bedroom. Rafe got up, went to her, and even though the heat was still stirring, he pulled her into his arms.

He didn't try to offer her a light at the end of the tunnel by saying—of course, Patricia would recover enough to be questioned. And, that Patricia would have an explanation for why she opened fire on them.

But that might not be true.

Sometimes, people had full psychotic breaks, and that could be what happened to the woman.

"Gavin and her kids are with their grandparents," Bree added. She didn't move out of his arms. She stayed there, resting her cheek on his shoulder. "Those kids have essentially lost both parents."

That was true, and again, he didn't offer up platitudes about kids being resilient and such. Because this would affect them, and down the road, they'd need the same answers that Bree needed now.

Such as why had their father died.

And why had their mother turned would-be killer?

"Someone provoked Patricia," Bree insisted, and she lifted her head to look at him. Eye to eye. Breath to breath. "I've put in a request to get her phone records, but it'll be tomorrow—"

"Jericho's already checked," he said. "She got and received multiple calls and texts from her parents and other family members. There were a couple of unanswered ones from Gavin's boss and friends."

"So, maybe someone in her family convinced Patricia that I'd killed her husband?" But she immediately shook her head, and her mouth tightened. "Buckner must have gotten to her somehow. Either a personal visit or even a letter that he planted for her to find."

"If it was a letter or such, she didn't report it to the SAPD cops," Rafe let her know. "Of course, depending on what was said in the letter, Patricia might have thought all cops were dirty."

Bree made a weary sound of agreement. "Maybe Buckner does have a dirty cop in his pocket. Perhaps someone tied to the investigation into Gavin's death." She lifted her phone, no doubt ready to make a call about that, but he gently put his hand over hers to stop her.

"My advice—let Jericho look into this. If you start asking about dirty cops, then SAPD might stop cooperating with you. You need them on your side right now since Gavin's death was in their jurisdiction."

He could tell she wanted to argue. That she wanted to do something now that would get her answers. But she sighed again, letting him know she understood he was right.

"Three people dead," Bree grumbled, moving away from him so she could pace across the room. "Two yet unidentified. Multiple injuries. I still have two deputies on mandatory bedrest." She squeezed her eyes shut a moment. "And I don't know why any of this is happening."

"Sure, you do," Rafe insisted. "Your cop's brain is spinning with the theory that starts with the bones. Someone killed that woman who might or might not be Tessa, and everything else that's happened since is to muddy the waters and cover up his or her crime."

She stopped pacing and stared at him. "Yes, that. But I don't know who."

"Buckner," he quickly provided. "There has to be a reason he's avoiding your calls."

"He could be dead like Gavin," she pointed out.

Rafe had gone there in his own theory and had dismissed it. "If Buckner's dead, then who else is pulling the strings? It would have to be someone who could get to him, and he doesn't impress me as the sort who'd let down his guard. Still, it's possible," he admitted after a pause. "And it's why Jericho is doing one of his deep dives into any and all of Buckner's family, friends, and acquaintances. If something is there, Jericho will find it."

Again, she looked as if she wanted to argue about that. Or about anything. He understood that, too. Exhaustion could create a restlessness. It could also lower barriers that shouldn't be lowered. He understood that when he saw the look in her eyes.

The heat.

Hell, it was there all right, and it was obvious from the set of her jaw, that she wasn't any happier about it than he was.

She cursed under her breath. "I should have never danced with you at that party," she grumbled.

Rafe nodded. "I consider that one of my turning points for you, too."

They stood there. Gazes locked. A whole hell of a lot of fire zinging between them. Fire he damn well knew he should be resisting.

But did he?

Nope.

Neither did Bree. She started toward him at the same moment he went to her. They met, both reaching for each other, and in a flash, she was in his arms.

And his mouth was on hers.

One touch of their lips and the taste of her roared through him. He hadn't needed anything else to make him senseless, but that did it. He lost all reason, and the only thought that was getting through his head was her.

Bree.

Just Bree.

The kiss was instantly scalding. So needy, so desperate that Rafe thought it could melt them on the spot. There was way too much pent-up lust in this for it to be happening, but the kiss raged on.

Their tongues met while she pressed her body against his. He'd been able to see all those curves beneath the PJs, but now he could feel them. Her breasts on his chest. And her center against his dick that thought this was a great time to go rock hard and ready.

But this wasn't a great time.

Not for the kiss. And not for where this kiss would lead them if they didn't stop. They would end up having adrenaline-fueled sex, which was sure to be amazing, but he didn't want Bree to have any regrets if they ever did become lovers. This would turn out to be a regret, no doubt about that.

Somehow, Rafe managed to pull back. *Somehow.* His dick and pretty much the rest of him protested that, but he forced himself not to listen to that primal need to sate this fire.

Bree moved back too, and with her breath gusting, she glanced around with a *WTF just happened* expression. He was right there right with her on that.

"Yes, that dance was a mistake," Bree muttered, making him laugh. Eventually, she smiled and then chuckled. "Who knew a few dance moves could start a spark like that?"

"It started before the dance," he said. At least he thought it was audible. Hard to tell with his heartbeat thundering in his ears. "It started back after high school. After Tessa and I began drifting apart."

She sighed. "It started before that," she admitted.

"It did," he was quick to verify. "I guess it just sounded less sleazy than saying I was going out with one woman and lusting after another."

Bree stayed quiet a moment, still making a visible attempt to level her breath. "Less sleazy than me wanting my blood friend's boyfriend. I did want you," she admitted in a mutter. "Still do." She stopped, cursed. What's going on here?" she asked.

Rafe knew she wasn't talking about the investigation. But rather that kiss. That scalding mistake of a kiss and all the lust and need that went along with it.

"Nothing's going on," he said, and he hoped he could make it true. "At least not until you've had a good night's sleep." To carry through on that, he went to her bed and pulled back the covers. "Rest," he insisted.

She slid some glances between the bed and him, her gaze lingering on him for several hot moments. Before she finally slipped between the covers.

Rafe didn't risk planting a chaste goodnight kiss on the uninjured part of her forehead. No kiss would stay chaste between Bree and him. So, he turned and forced himself out of the room.

As he eased the door shut behind him, Rafe had one

question pounding in his head.

How the hell was he going to stop himself from falling hard for Bree?

Chapter Eight

───── ☆ ─────

Bree woke with a jolt, the images of the nightmare still racing through her head. She tried to shake them off.

And then winced when she got a jab of pain.

She certainly hadn't forgotten about the stitches on her forehead, but they had announced themselves with the movement. She needed more pain meds. Needed to get up, too, she realized when she checked the time. Sweet heaven. It was nearly eight in the morning, well past her normal hour for starting her day.

Cursing under her breath, she threw back the covers, hurrying to the bathroom, and nearly came to a full stop as she remembered Rafe was in the house. In fact, he was in the guest room directly across the hall from her. Or rather that's where he was supposed to have slept anyway. It was likely he was already up and working on the investigation.

Since she'd showered the night before, Bree threw on her clothes. Wearing a uniform made that easy, and she had a line of them in her closet. She yanked on her boots and holster and then did her minimal grooming.

Today though, she paused to really see herself in the mirror.

Definitely not a beauty queen like Tessa. No makeup, and there were times, like now, when it looked as if she'd taken a go at cutting her own hair.

What the heck had Rafe seen in her?

And he must have seen, and felt, something to give her that scorcher of a kiss. Of course, she'd delivered an equally hot kiss to him, too. That didn't make it right. No. In fact, it'd been wrong because the timing was awful for such things. The trick now would be not to let it interfere with working together.

She tamped down her thoughts and headed for the hall while she glanced at her messages. But there weren't any. She sighed because that meant one of her deputies had purposely held them back, probably with the hopes that she'd get some sleep. Well, the sleep had been accomplished, but now she had to play catch up.

Bree glanced in the open door of the guestroom. No Rafe. The bed was already made, and there were no sounds of a bath or shower coming from the ensuite. However, there was the wonderful scent of coffee permeating the house, and she followed it down the stairs and to the kitchen.

There was coffee, all right. Rafe was sipping some while pouring over something on his phone. Reports, no doubt, that his team had been sending him.

"Morning," he said. He stood, went to her, and took hold of her shoulders while he studied her forehead. "There's Tylenol on the table," he let her know. "I figured you'd need something, and you can take it on an empty stomach."

"Thanks," she muttered.

Since she did indeed need it, Bree took two right away, washing them down with the cup of coffee Rafe had poured for her. Obviously, he recalled that she took it black because he hadn't added anything to it.

Bree thanked him again and opened her laptop that she kept on the counter. She immediately fired off a group email to all the day shift and reserve deputies, asking them for updates. By now, there should be info pouring in from the CSIs, the bomb squad, the hospital where Patricia was being held, and even SAPD since they were the primary investigators of Gavin's death.

"How long have you been up?" she asked, and she made the mistake of looking at him. Really looking.

Crap.

Bree hated that she felt the punch of heat at just seeing him. Those *drown in me* green eyes that had likely coaxed plenty of women to bed. The rumpled dark brown hair that made her itch to run her fingers through it. And the face. Definitely not pretty. But rugged and hot. So. Very. Hot.

Again, the timing for this sucked.

Rafe stared at her as she was staring at him, and he seemed to develop mind-reading skills. Either that or she was showing the lust on her face. She glanced away just so she'd stand a chance of cooling down her body.

"I've been up about two hours. I tried not to make any noise so you could sleep in, though I figure you won't thank me for that," he added, flashing her a smile.

A real, actual smile.

She'd forgotten just how much more amazing it could make his face that was already too amazing as it was.

"No, I won't thank you," she muttered. "We have way too much to do today for me to be sleeping in."

And apparently, her deputies had been waiting for her to acknowledge she was awake because the emails came flooding in.

"Both Alice and Carson are doing well," she relayed to him. "They'll still be on quarters for today and maybe tomorrow, but they're on the mend."

She went to the next report. "Teddy Sanchez from the bomb squad says the explosive device wasn't complicated. Bottom line—plenty of people could have constructed it with just info they got off the Internet."

Rafe made a sound to let her know he'd anticipated that. "Sanchez has sent the remains of the device to the lab, so we still might get something." He put two pieces of bread into the toaster.

Might was the best they could hope for on that, so she moved on to the next report from Millie. "Patricia is being weaned off sedation today, but her doctor is refusing to let anyone other than medical staff near her."

For a second, Bree contemplated asking Rafe if his boss would have any pull in that particular area, but she immediately nixed the idea. Best to stick to the letter of the law. If Patricia was eventually deemed fit to stand trial, then the charges and the evidence had to be clean.

Of course, the "cleanest" part of that would be

multiple eyewitness accounts to her attempting to gun down a cop. That could potentially land the woman in jail for decades. But Bree took no pleasure in that since she believed all the way down to the soles of her boots that Patricia had been manipulated into firing those shots.

The toast popped up just as her phone rang, and when she saw Ollie's name on the screen, she put the call on speaker. "Please tell me you have good news," Bree greeted.

"I've got an ID on our dead woman," he was quick to say. "Dani Dawson." He spelled that out for them, and Rafe immediately began typing something on his phone.

"The name doesn't sound familiar," Bree said to Ollie. "How were you able to ID her?"

"Fingerprints. She was in the system for a DUI from two years ago. And that's all I have on her for now. I just got the ID a couple of minutes ago and figured you'd want to know."

"You figured right," she assured him just as Rafe lifted his phone and showed her the photo of an attractive blonde woman. The man was fast.

"She's thirty-nine," Rafe provided, turning his phone back so he could read off what he'd accessed. "She's a waitress at the Tip Top Café in San Antonio. Her address is in San Antonio, too, and her next of kin is her stepfather, Barney Salvetti." He looked at Bree. "I have his address and contact info if you're doing the death notification."

"I am," she said. Then, she amended that to, "We are." They'd want to question the stepfather to get any info that would explain why Dani had ended up dead and dumped at the inn.

"Ollie, do you have any idea yet how she died?" Bree continued.

"A blow to the temple," he was quick to say. "I'm guessing with some kind of blunt object. All the other trauma to the body was post-mortem."

"The temple," Rafe said, and even though he'd practically muttered it, Ollie must have heard.

"Yeah," Ollie responded. "And it's in the nearly identical spot to the victim in the grave. I'll let you draw your own conclusions from that since the best I can do is speculate that it's possible a person of the same height and strength killed both women, but of course, there's no way to know."

"No way," she muttered. "Not without more evidence."

She heard Ollie draw in a long breath. "I had a conversation with the forensic anthropologist about that late last night, and she couldn't do more than agree with my speculation about the similarity of the two wounds," he went on. "By the way, she said she should have the DNA results back on those bones this morning so she will be calling you soon."

Good. Then, maybe they'd have both women positively identified, and they could start threading together any connections.

"The only other things I can tell you on Dani Dawson

is she's never had a child and was in reasonably good health before someone ended her life," Ollie went on. "Her last meal was nachos and beer. She wasn't drunk," he added. "Since she'd been dead in my estimation for less than forty-eight hours, I was able to test..." He stopped. "You really don't want to hear about femoral veins, do you?"

"I don't," Bree verified. She didn't get queasy by such things, but she trusted Ollie to know what he was doing. "If she wasn't over the legal limit, that's all I need to know about blood alcohol levels. Anything else?"

"Not unless some of the lab work comes back with surprises, but I really don't expect any. Everything I saw in the autopsy pointed to a woman who'd been killed with a single blow to the head. No defensive bruises, no broken bones."

"So, someone walked up to her and clubbed her," Bree concluded. She could guess that meant Dani had known her attacker, but it was possible she'd been bashed while sleeping. "Face to face or from the side?"

"I'd say face to face from someone who's right-handed. If it'd been an accidental fall with her hitting her head, I'd expect a different angle," Ollie spelled out to her. "Any other questions?"

"No, that should do it for now."

"All right. Then, I'll put all of this in a report and fire it off to you." Ollie paused a heartbeat. "You'll let me know if the other victim is Tessa?"

"I will," she assured him. She thanked him and ended

the call. The moment she turned back to Rafe, she realized he'd already discovered something. "What?" she couldn't ask fast enough.

"Dani used to work as a cocktail waitress at the San Antonio bar that Buckner owns," Rafe spelled out.

"Holy crap," she muttered. She sank down onto one of the counter stools next to him so she could read the report on his phone.

"She stopped working there about a month ago," Rafe pointed out, "but before that, she'd worked for him since the bar opened. That would have been less than a year after Tessa disappeared."

Bree tried to process that. "So, she was a long-term employee. I don't guess you know why she quit or was fired?"

"Not yet, but Jericho's on it, so we should have something soon."

"Good," she muttered, taking out her phone again. Like Ollie, she already had plenty of faith in Jericho's abilities to do his job. And apparently part of his job was digging up info fast.

She called Detective Malley at SAPD. He didn't answer, but she left him a message, asking him to help her find Buckner, that the man could be linked to at least one of the dead women. Possibly to both if Davy had been right in thinking the man he'd seen with Tessa all those years ago could have been Buckner.

"If Malley doesn't get back to me soon, I want to do

that trip to San Antonio to try to find Buckner myself."

It could end up being a waste of time if the man was truly dodging them, but she needed to see him. Of course, she also needed to do the death notification and question Dani's stepfather.

Her sigh must have alerted Rafe that her day already felt too jammed-packed because he stood. For a moment—one heart-racing moment—she thought he was going to pull her back into his arms for what would no doubt be a mistake hug.

Or another mistake kiss.

But instead, he went to the toaster, put the two pieces of toast on a plate and set them on the counter. "Unless your eating habits have changed, I seem to remember you preferring a light breakfast."

"Or no breakfast at all," she said.

He nodded. "You like to fuel up on coffee all morning, but you might need a carb boost."

"You might need one as well." She picked up a piece of toast and held it out for him.

For some reason, their gazes locked, and Bree could have sworn that actual heat speared out between them. That caused her to sigh again.

It caused him to smile.

Oh, she so did not need that sex-on-the-counter grin from him this morning. Not when her body was urging her there was something a whole lot better than a carb boost. A Rafe boost would work so very well.

His ESP must have kicked up again because he leaned in and brushed a kiss on her mouth. "Playing with fire," he drawled, doing another touch of his lips to hers. "Running with scissors. Tearing tags off mattresses."

She laughed. Which, after looking at him, was what he'd intended. Rafe knew this was indeed a distraction that could hurt the investigation.

Heck, it could hurt everything.

And this was his attempt to rein it in. She wasn't sure he was successful, but at least the kiss hadn't gone full-blown. Even if it had though, it wouldn't have lasted long because her phone rang.

Bree was hoping it was Detective Malley, but she didn't recognize the number on the screen. She answered it though and put it on speaker. "This is Sheriff O'Neil," she said.

"Sheriff, I'm Addison Kreppner, the forensic anthro. I'm guessing Rafe is with you, so I can brief you both at once."

"He's here and listening," Bree assured her, and judging from the fact the woman had used his given name, that likely meant they knew each other.

"After studying the remains and the DNA, I don't believe this body is a match for Tessa Wainwright," Dr. Kreppner said in a no-nonsense tone.

That knocked some of the air out of her, and Bree had to take a moment to steady herself. Even though she had known this outcome was a possibility, it still came as a shock. A good shock.

"Tessa's alive," Bree muttered.

"I can't say one way or another on that," the doctor commented. "But I'm positive these are not her bones. The height is off for one thing, and neither this woman's shoe nor clothes' sizes match Tessa's. Ruby got me that info," she added. "She asked Wade to go through Tessa's closet. Tessa wore a size six shoe and size four dress. This woman, a size eight shoe and approximately a dress size of ten."

That was indeed a big enough size difference to indicate it wasn't Tessa.

"But there is a familial match," the doctor tacked onto that after a short pause.

"Familial match?" Bree had to shake her head. "What does that mean exactly?"

"It means this woman you recovered from the grave was related to Tessa's father. I'm guessing this is his child. Or if he had an identical twin brother, it's possible it could be Wade's niece."

"Tessa didn't have any sisters," Bree muttered, and she looked at Rafe for confirmation of that.

He nodded.

But a child of Wade's twin was possible. Still, Bree couldn't recall Tessa ever mentioning a close uncle or cousins. Just the opposite. Tessa had often complained about not having a big family and being an only child, something that hadn't gotten a lot of sympathy from Rafe or Bree since they both had younger siblings.

"Do you have an estimate for how long the woman's

been dead?" Bree pressed.

"An estimate," the doctor emphasized. "More than fifteen years but less than twenty."

So, that would fit the time frame for when Tessa disappeared. But were the death and the disappearance connected?

Bree knew that was something the doctor wouldn't be able to tell her. To get that answer, she'd need to find out who the dead woman was and work backwards.

"They recovered enough of the bones for me to indicate the woman was five six," the doctor continued. "With a few more tests, I'll be able to get her eye and hair color in case you need that to narrow down some possibilities. But for now, I'd say look for a woman in her late teens or early twenties who went missing fifteen to twenty years ago."

A possible teenager. That was another gut punch, and judging from the throaty sound Rafe made, he felt the same way.

"Your ME was right," the doctor went on, "Other than the blow to the head, no other injuries. I can't even find a previously healed broken bone, and judging from the remains, she hadn't been dealing with any obvious medical issues."

So, she likely hadn't suffered. Not before death anyway. But Bree got an image of a teenage girl moaning in pain as she bled out from a blow to the head.

"What about the teeth?" Rafe asked. "Did that give

you any clues as to her identity?"

"No," the doctor was quick to say. "As you know, the dental databases are only useful if the missing person's dental records have been uploaded. Hers weren't. That's possibly because the databases weren't around when she disappeared. Or if she went missing from say a small town, they might not have had the knowledge or resources for the upload."

Bree wasn't offended by that. Even though she made sure she and her deputies kept up with their training, new technologies popped up all the time, and sometimes the info didn't trickle down to rural areas.

"She didn't go missing from here," Bree assured the doctor. "A missing woman or a runaway wouldn't stay a secret for long."

Rafe made a quick sound of agreement, and he got to work on his phone again. He was no doubt plugging in all the pieces of info that Dr. Kreppner had just doled out to them.

"One last thing," the doctor added. "I checked with the lab tech who has the leather coat. Rafe had indicated it was probably custom-made, and I wanted to see if there was a date or initials stitched into it. Some tailors do that, but no such luck on this one. But the tech pointed out that, in his opinion, the jacket hadn't been worn much, that it was possibly new at the time it went into that grave."

Interesting since Tessa's jacket was far from new. It was several years old, and Bree recalled that once the lining had to be repaired when Tessa had snagged it on something. Bree would relay that to the lab. However, the moment she put that on her mental to-do list, Rafe pointed to his phone to let her know he was already on that.

"Thank you for this," Bree told the doctor, and once they'd said their goodbyes, she hung up and looked at Rafe. "If I could afford you, you'd make a really good assistant."

He smiled. Not for long though. Probably because he knew what they had to do next. "You want me to text Wade and ask him for a meeting, or do you want to do that yourself?"

"I'll do it." She paused, considering how this could all play out. She would be giving Wade the good news that it wasn't his daughter's bones, but that another family member was dead. Bree had no idea how Wade would handle that news or handle the big question she would have to ask.

Was this dead woman or girl his bio-child?

"I'll ask Wade to come here," she muttered while she composed the text. "Best to do this away from the station."

He made another of those sounds of agreement and continued typing on his own phone. Hopefully, getting them some answers even before Wade arrived.

Shortly after sending the text, she got a response back from Wade, saying he was on his way. Only seconds after that, her doorbell rang.

Bree groaned. No way was it Wade already. She hoped it wasn't a neighbor coming over to pump her for info about the investigation.

"I'll go with you to the door," Rafe insisted.

She certainly hadn't forgotten about the explosion or the fact that someone might want to cover up an old murder. But seeing Rafe morph into the special ops mode made her up her own stance. She adjusted her body in case she had to draw the gun in her shoulder holster.

They stopped at the door, but Rafe didn't look out the peephole. Instead, he went to the front window and peered out the side.

Then, he muttered some profanity.

"I'm pretty sure Buckner and two goons are standing on your porch," Rafe informed her.

"Is he armed?" she asked.

"No visible weapon. The two thugs are carrying concealed beneath their jackets."

So, Buckner had brought some backup with him, but Bree had her own backup, and she waited until Rafe had stepped right by her side.

Before she opened the door to a possible killer.

Chapter Nine

☆

Rafe's every instinct was to move in front of Bree. To protect her from this potential threat. But she was a cop, and there was no way she would appreciate his playing hero. That didn't mean though that he wouldn't step up if the situation called for it.

One look at Buckner and Rafe thought it might call for it.

His impression was the same as when he'd first seen Buckner's photo. The man looked like a seedy criminal with a thin veneer of polish. Just enough polish and possible charm that he could have lured someone like Tessa right in.

And then maybe killed her.

Maybe killed Dani and the unidentified woman as well. Rafe didn't know how yet, but everything was connected to this one asshole who was now inches away from Bree and him.

An oily smile stretched across Buckner's mouth, and he extended his hand to Bree. "I'm Callum Buckner," he said. "And if you're Sheriff Bree O'Neil, I understand you've been looking for me."

"Yes," Bree verified, her voice edged with ice. "I didn't expect you to come to my home though. How'd you find out where I live?"

"I keep a really good PI on retainer," Buckner

answered. "I can give you his name if you like."

There was ice in Buckner's voice, too, but he was coating it with more of that damn veneer. Rafe rarely despised someone on sight, but he made an exception in this guy's case.

"No, thank you," Bree fired back. "I wanted to question you about...a lot of things."

Buckner outstretched his hands in a cocky *here I am* gesture. "I'm in between appointments and can spare you a half hour. I suppose we could eat up some of that time by driving to the police station, or you can just ask your questions now." He fanned the side of his jacket. "Though it's leaning toward hotter than hell out here, so let's do it inside."

Buckner looked at Rafe then as if just noticing him. Another façade. The man had noticed him all right and had already sized him up. Ditto for the two muscled goons who stood just behind Buckner.

"Callum Buckner," he said, extending a hand to Rafe.

He didn't shake it. "Rafe Cross."

Buckner's eyes widened, and he dropped back a step while pressing his hand to his heart. "Boys, we're in the presence of a celebrity. This is *the* Rafe Cross from Maverick Ops. He works for Ruby Maverick."

"You know Ruby?" he asked.

"I know of her. Know of you, too," Buckner added.

For just a moment, the veneer slipped, and Rafe saw the slime behind it. The disappointment, too. Maybe

Buckner had thought he could come here and intimidate Bree if she'd been alone. But the man clearly didn't know Bree. She wasn't the sort for intimidation.

"You can come inside and talk," Bree finally said to Buckner. "Only you. Your employees can wait outside."

Buckner looked ready to argue that, but then he shrugged. "Wait in the truck," he muttered to them. "I won't be long. And if I need protection, I've got the celebrity Rafe Cross for that."

Obviously, Buckner had heard some things, maybe about Rafe's missions. More likely though he'd "heard" those things from that PI he kept on retainer. By now, Buckner probably knew a hell of a lot more about Bree and him than they did about him.

That was about to change.

Bree showed him in, motioning for him to take a seat in one of the chairs in the living room. She sat across from him on the sofa. Rafe stayed standing, positioning himself so he could keep an eye on Buckner and the goons. From the window, he saw the two men leaning against the truck, and they had their attention pinned to the house. One sound of trouble, and they'd no doubt rush right in.

"Hope you don't mind me pointing this out," Buckner commented, "but you two look like you've had the shit beat out of you. Those are some serious bruises and cuts. Did that happen in the explosion I heard about?"

"How did you hear about that?" Rafe wanted to know.

"The PI. That man is a regular font of information."

His voice was laced with sarcasm.

"I'm going to Mirandize you," Bree interrupted, and before Buckner could respond, she started reading him his rights. Buckner tried to seem amused by it, but there was that sliver of real emotion again. Fury, this time. "Would you like to have your lawyer present?" she tacked onto the reciting. "You probably have a really good one on retainer."

Rafe didn't bother to hold back a smile. And he let Buckner see it, too.

Another sliver of anger.

Maybe if there were enough slivers, the man would erupt and say something that would get him locked up for life. Like confessing to a murder or two.

"I won't call my lawyer. For now," Buckner said. "This is just a friendly conversation, right?"

Bree hit the recorder function on her phone and placed it on the coffee table between them. "Sure," she muttered, stating the time, date, location, and the names of those present. "Mr. Buckner, for the record, you're waiving your right to have an attorney present at this interview. Please give a verbal response so it'll be on the recording."

"Yes." Short and not so sweet.

"And the recording," Bree prompted. "Do you consent to that as well as having consultant, Rafe Cross, sit in on the interview and ask you questions that could help us with our inquiry?"

The muscles worked in his throat. "Sure. Why not? I've got nothing to hide. Yes, to no lawyer. Yes, to the recording.

Yes, to celebrity Rafe putting in his two cents worth with questions."

"Good. Thank you." In contrast, Bree's voice was calm and professional.

"Hey, are you two going to play good cop, bad cop?" Buckner asked. "If so, I'm betting he's the bad cop." He hiked his thumb toward Rafe before shifting back to Bree. "And you can do the whole I'm on your side role."

"I wouldn't count on that," Rafe muttered. No need to add the rest to that, that neither Bree nor he were on this man's side.

"Oh, well," Buckner remarked. "Then, bring it on. Both of you go all hard ass on me."

Rafe didn't react to that. Neither did Bree.

"Mr. Buckner, tell me about your relationship with Dani Dawson," Bree began.

"Dani?" Buckner pulled back his shoulders, either surprised or pretending to be. "She used to work for me. What about her?"

"Used to work for you?" Bree repeated.

"Yeah, she quit last month." He leaned back, stretching his arms across the back of the sofa. "It's a shame because Dani was a damn good worker, and I haven't been able to replace her."

"Why'd she quit?" she pressed.

"Don't I wish I knew. She wouldn't say. Told me she had some personal things she had to work out. Probably with that loser she'd been seeing."

Rafe jumped in on that. "A boyfriend?"

"If you can call him that," Buckner grumbled. "More like a dickwad loser. She deserved better, and I told her so."

"What's his name?" Bree asked.

Buckner blew out a breath, and his forehead bunched up. "Not sure. She called him Honey Bear."

Bree gave him a flat look. "That doesn't sound like a dickwad loser's nickname to me."

"No accounting for some things. I guess he must have had some redeeming qualities. I only saw the guy twice, and both times he came into the bar and accused Dani of fucking other guys. He caused a scene, and I had to get one of my bouncers to toss him out."

"Did Dani admit to seeing other men?" Rafe asked.

"No way. She claimed she was devoted to him and all. But on one of those occasions, when Dani came into work the next morning, she was sporting a black eye." He leaned forward as if revealing a secret. "Let me tell you, no amount of Maybelline was going to cover that shit. Honey Bear must have had a go at her."

Rafe considered texting Jericho to get him to look into Dani's personal relationships, including this one, but Jericho was likely already doing that. If not, Rafe could fill him in after the interview. For now, he wanted to keep his attention on Buckner and the goons who were still by the truck.

"Why are you asking me about Dani?" Buckner demanded. "Did something happen to her?"

No way would Bree spill anything about Dani being dead, not until the next of kin had been notified. "Did you know Tessa Wainwright?" she continued, obviously moving onto the next subject.

Again, Buckner did one of those eyes wide, mental double take expressions. "Tessa Wainwright?" He sat back and smiled. "Now, that's a blast from the past, all right." He repeated her name several times, his smile widening with each repeat. "Where the heck is she?"

"So, you know her?" Bree commented.

"Hell, yeah, I know her. Well, I knew her anyway. Haven't seen her in…must be nearly twenty years." He stopped. "Hey, she disappeared for a while. Where'd she end up? I'd love to see her and catch up."

"When exactly was the last time you saw Tessa?" Bree, again.

"Like I said, it has to be close to twenty years. Why?"

"We need to narrow down some timelines." Bree didn't add more. She just stared at Buckner and waited.

"All right, let me see," he muttered after an annoyed huff. "She had already flunked out of college the last time I saw her so that would mean she was about twenty. Does that sound right?" he asked, directing the question to Rafe. "I mean, you were her go-to guy."

Rafe had no idea what the hell that meant, and he wasn't going to press him on it. But it was interesting that even after all this time, Buckner could recall that Tessa had been involved with him.

Buckner huffed again. "Okay, let's assume Tessa was twenty then, and since I'm a year older than her, that would make eighteen years since I last saw her."

"And how long after that did you hear she was missing?" Rafe piped in.

Buckner gave them both hard looks. "Did something happen to Tessa?" But he instantly waved that off. "Since you haven't answered shit so far, I should save my breath and quit asking stuff." He checked the time on his Rolex. "How much longer will this interview last?"

"Until we have the information we need," Bree calmly replied. "But hopefully you'll be forthcoming with what we want to know so you won't have to be here much longer."

That didn't exactly please Buckner, but he made an impatient, get on with it gesture with his hand.

"You said you last saw Tessa approximately eighteen years ago," Bree reminded him. "When did you learn she was missing?"

Sighing as if it were the most tedious question in history, he put his hand to his forehead, rubbing his temples with his thumb and ring finger. "Probably shortly thereafter. I remember calling her and not getting an answer, so I thought she'd maybe ghosted me. Then, somebody told me she was missing."

"Who?" Rafe pressed.

"How the hell do you expect me to remember that?" Buckner fired back. "Eighteen years. I'll bet you can't recall when you last saw her or how you found out she was missing."

"Eighteen years, one month and eleven days ago," Rafe said, quickly doing the math. "And I found out from her father, Wade Wainwright."

Buckner rolled his eyes. "Well, obviously you cared about her a whole lot more than I did. Look, man, she was just a good fuck, that's it." He added a grin, probably hoping it would provoke Rafe.

It didn't. Yes, once he'd loved Tessa, but right now, he only wanted to learn her fate. And he probably wouldn't be learning it from this clown.

If Buckner had murdered her and those other women, no way would he be fessing up to that. And if he hadn't killed her, then it was possible he was telling the truth and that Tessa was no longer on his radar. Bree must have realized that, too, because she moved on to the next item on the agenda.

"Tell me about Gavin McCray," she threw out there.

No smile or look of surprise, but something did go through his eyes. Worry, maybe. But it was barely a flash of it, and it was gone as quickly as it'd come.

"Gavin, the construction guy," Buckner said. "Yeah, he did a private job for me at my place."

"What kind of job?" Bree asked.

"A koi pond," the man said after a short pause. "He did it off the books so I paid him in cash."

Bree didn't show any disappointment, but Rafe figured she had to be. If Buckner had tried to lie his way out of this by denying he knew Gavin, it could be enough to charge him at least with obstruction of justice.

"Do you have photos of the koi pond?" Rafe pressed. "Or maybe we can go to your place and see it?"

Buckner cursed. "It's not built yet so there's nothing to see."

"But you said Mr. McCray did a private job for you," Bree pointed out.

"Then, I misspoke. I meant to say he *planned* a private job." He paused again. "I paid him an advance so he could get the supplies, and I plan to pay him the rest once he's finished it."

"Mr. McCray won't be able to finish it," Bree said. "Because he's dead."

Buckner went through his stunned act. And Rafe was certain now that it was just that. An act.

"Dead?" Buckner repeated. "How? Was it in that explosion?"

"Cause of his death is still to be determined," Bree answered, and like Rafe, she pinned her attention to Buckner, looking for any hint that he was pissed that it hadn't been ruled a suicide.

"Well, that's a damn shame he's dead," Buckner muttered, and he stood while checking his watch. "I need to be heading out."

"It hasn't been thirty minutes," Rafe volunteered.

"Yeah, but I hadn't factored in just how long it could take me to get back to San Antonio. Sometimes, there are tractors and shit on the road that leads to the Interstate." He turned to Bree. "I'm afraid if there are any more questions, we'll have to schedule them for another time."

"This afternoon at one," Bree suggested, and then she read the time the interview had been terminated into the recording.

"Sorry. No can do," Buckner said, heading for the door. "Tell you what, I'll have my assistant call you and set up a time." He fished out his wallet and handed Bree a business card.

When Buckner threw open the door, Rafe saw the two thugs jump into action to come toward their boss. He also saw Wade's approaching silver Ford Raptor truck.

"Looks like you got another visitor anyway," Buckner added under his breath. He froze though when Wade stepped out. "You can ask Tessa's daddy all the questions about her you just asked me."

"You know Wade Wainwright?" Rafe asked, latching right onto that.

Buckner didn't exactly flinch, but it was close. "No. I mean, we've never met, but I recall seeing a picture of him."

"In his house? In Tessa's room?" Rafe pressed.

Buckner's eyes narrowed. "I said any other questions would have to wait." And with that, he barreled down the steps.

Wade and Buckner exchanged nodded greetings as they passed each other, but Wade didn't seem to recognize the man. Instead, Wade had his focus on Bree and him.

"Did something happen?" Wade asked before he even reached them. "Are the bones Tessa's?"

Bree gently took hold of Wade's arm, leading him into the house. Rafe stayed on the porch a few seconds longer, staring down Buckner and his thugs. Buckner glared at him as they drove off.

Yes, Buckner definitely needed to be questioned again.

"Don't make me wait," Rafe heard Wade say when he came back into the house. "Just tell me. I need to know if my baby girl is truly gone."

"Neither the bones nor the body is Tessa's," Bree said.

Wade stared at her, and then the breath seemed to rush out of his body. He dropped down onto the sofa. "Not Tessa," he muttered over and over again.

Rafe went to the kitchen and brought Wade back a glass of water. Wade downed the entire glass like a man dying of thirst.

"Thank you," Wade muttered. He said nothing else for a long time. "If Tessa's not dead, then where is she?"

That was a good question. But not the one Rafe had been expecting. He'd thought Wade would want to know who'd been buried in that grave, but maybe this was a sort of paternal tunnel vision. Perhaps the only thing he could think of right now was his daughter.

"I don't know where Tessa is," Rafe spelled out. "How long has it been since you looked for her?"

"Years," Wade admitted. He shook his head as if disgusted by that, and he lifted his tear filled eyes to Rafe.

"She sent me a postcard I didn't tell you about. It said, *Stop looking for me.* That was it. No, *I love you, Daddy.* No, *I'm okay.* Just that, *Stop looking for me.* I figured that meant she wanted nothing to do with me."

Rafe could see that had ripped Wade to pieces.

"Do you know why Tessa would write something like that to me?" Wade pled, volleying glances at both of them.

"No," Rafe said, and Bree shook her head. "I just assumed she was embarrassed at flunking out of college," Rafe added. "Or that maybe she wanted a clean break."

"Yeah," Wade muttered. "I figured those things, too, but I always guessed she'd come back and explain why she did what she did. And then when I thought those were her bones, I said to myself—well, that's why she hasn't returned. She couldn't. Coming back was a choice that was taken away from her because somebody killed her."

Rafe could understand that logic. Again, it was a coping mechanism. But not knowing had to be hard as hell, too.

"I'll start looking for her again," Wade said after another long silence. "Maybe I can even hire Ruby Maverick and your team. If anybody can find Tessa, Maverick Ops can."

That was true. But the truth might end up being a bitter pill to swallow since it was indeed possible that Tessa was dead.

Bree touched Wade's arm to get his attention. "Wade, about those bones we found. The forensic anthropologist believes the dead woman is a relative of Tessa's. A familial match like a half sibling or a first cousin."

The color drained from Wade's face. "A relative? Who?"

"We don't know," Bree said. "Any idea who she could be?"

He shook his head and seemed still caught up in the emotion of learning that his baby girl could still be alive. "Tessa's an only child."

"Is it possible you fathered a child you don't know about?" Bree pressed, and Rafe could tell she had dreaded bringing this up. But it had to be asked. "A daughter who would have been a couple of years younger than Tessa?"

"I don't have any other children," Wade was quick to say, and he seemed to be searching for possibilities that would cause this to make sense. "But I have an uncle. I'm not close with him, haven't seen him in years, and he's got kids. I can ask him."

Bree didn't think that would be enough to create this kind of familial connection. Any children from Wade's uncle would be Tessa's second cousins.

"Oh, and my mom had an identical twin sister, Aunt Ida, who married a man who was also an identical twin. They had a child, a daughter, I believe. Both Ida and her husband died young, but their daughter would be pretty close kin to Tessa, right?"

"Possibly," Bree conceded. "Could you give us their full names and a way to get in touch with their next of kin? And any other relative you can think of who might match?"

"I will," Wade assured her. "I have to go," he said, standing. "I need, uh...I just need to go."

"I understand," Bree assured him, and they walked with him to the door.

"Do you still have the postcard Tessa sent you?" Rafe asked him.

"Of course." Wade's voice barely had any sound. "It was all I had of my baby girl for so long. Why? Did you keep yours?"

"Unfortunately, no," Rafe had to admit. "When I was on deployment, the storage facility with my things burned, and I lost everything in it. But if you have the postcard, it could be processed for prints or some other evidence that might tell us where Tessa is."

It was a long shot, but if Buckner's prints were on the postcard, it could mean Buckner had not only sent it but also murdered Tessa. If so though, where was her body? Or was she truly still alive and out there somewhere?

Wade's eyes brightened a little. "Yes. I hadn't thought of that, of the postcard giving us some clues. But, yes. I have them at home. I'll put it in a plastic bag and have someone bring it to you."

"Use this." Tessa got up, went to one of the drawers in the kitchen and came back with an evidence bag. "The postcard will already have a lot of contamination on it, but this will save it from getting more."

True. In fact, plenty of people had likely handled that

postcard already. Still, an evidence bag could maybe prevent fingerprints from being smeared.

"Have it brought to the police station," Rafe instructed Wade. "Then, I'll get them to Ruby right away and see if she can work some of her magic."

That brightened his eyes even more, and Wade actually gave them both hugs before he headed back to his truck.

"Maybe the bones belong to this child from the aunt that Wade mentioned," Bree said as they went back inside.

Rafe was already taking out his phone to do a search on that and to alert Ruby to the incoming postcard that he'd have couriered to her. Ruby's place was over an hour away, and Rafe didn't want to take the time to go there today. Not when Bree was already gathering her things to head to the police station.

"On the drive into work, I'll contact Buckner's lawyer and arrange for another interview," Bree said, grabbing her keys. "Hopefully, today."

Rafe doubted that. He figured Buckner wasn't going to be so cooperative for a second round of questioning. The man had to know they suspected him of something. Murder, even.

Rafe followed Bree to the garage where she'd parked the cruiser, and he'd just fired off the text to Ruby when his phone rang.

"It's Jericho," he let her know. "You're on speaker," he added to Jericho.

"Good because I've got two things you'll both want to

hear. First, Honey Bear. And might I say, as terms of affection go, that's both sappy sweet and a little disturbing. Anyway, Honey Bear's real name is Craig Merkins, a former Green Beret who got booted for insubordination and ended up a bouncer."

"At Buckner's bar?" Bree asked, slipping behind the wheel of the cruiser. Rafe rode shotgun.

"Nope. In fact, Honey Bear has trouble keeping a job so he's floated around a lot. He's got anger management issues, a possible drinking problem, and tends to rant a lot on Facebook about how much his life stinks." Jericho paused. "But there's no way he killed Dani Dawson."

Bree groaned. From Jericho's description, she probably thought she'd be bringing in Honey Bear on a murder charge. "How do you know he didn't do it? Is he dead, too?"

"No. He's been in jail for the past three weeks. He got into a fight over a fender bender, drew an illegal weapon, and ended up taking a shot at a cop. Said cop naturally got really pissed off and charged him with a whole host of things, including attempted murder of a police officer. Honey Bear won't be going anywhere for a while."

Didn't sound like he would be. "Any signs this guy had the connections to have Dani killed?"

"None whatsoever. He's flat-assed broke, and people don't seem to like him enough to do any favors for him. Especially a favor that big. So, that probably takes you back to Dani's boss, Buckner."

"It does indeed," Bree verified, pulling out of the garage. "My gut feel is he's guilty of something. I just don't know what yet."

"Well, I'll keep digging and see if I can turn up some dirt," Jericho commented. "And that brings me to the second reason I'm calling. We have an ID on the skeletal remains."

Bree hit the brakes, stopping the car in her driveway. "Who is she?"

"Sandy Lynn Franklin. She went missing eighteen years ago on her twentieth birthday. And are you ready for the punchline here?" Jericho didn't wait for them to answer. "The DNA techs did a whole bunch more tests, and they've concluded that Sandy Lynn is definitely Wade Wainwright's daughter."

Chapter Ten

———— ☆ ————

With the dread building in her with each passing second, Bree threaded the cruiser down the country road while Rafe was reading through the latest report he'd gotten.

A thorough background check on Dani Dawson.

So far, he wasn't saying much, which meant there likely wasn't anything in it they could use to try to pin her murder on Buckner. If there was nothing to find, then they'd have to rely on other things. Such as canvassing the area around the inn/body dump and showing Buckner's photo to anyone who might have seen the man. That would be a huge drain on her manpower, but it was the next logical step since there were no traffic cameras on that particular stretch of the road.

The dread went up another notch when she took the turn to Wade's estate. She knew he was home because she'd called his housekeeper to confirm it. The housekeeper had told Bree that Wade had been in his office since he arrived back home.

It didn't sit well with her, but she had to face the possibility that the man had outright lied to them about Sandy Lynn being his daughter.

Of course, she was hoping that Wade hadn't known it was a lie.

That he hadn't been aware he'd fathered a child other

than Tessa.

Though, judging from the age the forensic anthropologist had determined, this child, this daughter, would have been born when Wade had been married. Around the time Tessa would have likely been a toddler. Certainly, if Wade had had an affair, he must have at least considered he could have gotten his lover pregnant.

She'd checked, and the DNA results were solid on this. Wade was definitely the dead woman's father, and the dead woman wasn't Tessa. That had been ruled out because of the height and size difference. So, who was Sandy Lynn, and why had her body been buried in Canyon Ridge?

Maybe the universe wanted to supply her with some answers to those questions because Rafe's phone sounded again with an incoming message.

"The preliminary background on Sandy Lynn," he said.

That was fast since Jericho and Ruby had only gotten the "tasking" for the background checks less than a half hour earlier.

"Good. Read it to me," she insisted. And she hoped the reading wouldn't take more than a minute or two since they'd soon be at Wade's.

"Sandy Lynn's mother is Nancy Franklin, aged fifty-seven, which means she was nineteen when she had Sandy Lynn. No father is listed on the birth certificate."

That didn't surprise Bree. In Texas, the father couldn't be listed unless he signed the certificate form or else the mother provided a court document proving paternity.

"Nancy listed her occupation as a waitress at a diner in San Antonio at the time of the delivery," Rafe went on. "Jericho's doing a background check on her now, and he's pretty sure she's still alive since there's no death certificate. Once he finds her...well, she'll need to know about her daughter."

"Yes," Bree agreed, which meant a death notification. A second one since she also had to notify Dani's stepfather.

"Now, onto Sandy Lynn," Rafe continued. "Jericho said everything he's got is still preliminary, but he'll keep digging. No criminal record. She won some academic awards and was runner-up in state cross country."

"So, not a troubled kid. Not on the surface anyway."

"Agreed. But Jericho and Ruby will find anything there is to find." He paused and kept reading. "After high school, she attended UT in Austin on scholarship. No major declared, that might be standard, but she was taking a lot of courses that indicate she was going for a degree in business."

Ironically, that'd been Tessa's major, though Wade had heavily influenced that. Tessa had wanted to be a fashion designer.

"Jericho located some old social media archives," Rafe went on, "and Sandy Lynn seemed like a typical teen, interested in boys and music."

Bree reached the gates to the estate and stopped. This time, she kept the cruiser back from the security camera, though it was possible some sensor had already alerted Wade to their arrival.

"Not everyone apparently loved Sandy Lynn though, since there were some digs from other teens on her posts about her having her nose stuck up in the air. Some called her a fake pretty, pretty princess, whatever the hell that means," Rafe added in a mutter.

"Interesting," Bree remarked. She had no idea what it meant either, but it told her that Sandy Lynn had interactions with people who didn't care much for her. Maybe one of them had killed her. "Are there photos in the archives?"

"Tons," Rafe verified, "and Jericho included some. Here's the one he found that was taken shortly before she disappeared."

He lifted his phone to show her the perky—yes, perky—blonde who very much resembled Tessa. Same hair color, the eye shape was the same. It was obvious they had some DNA in common.

And that got Bree thinking.

"Sandy Lynn would have been a freshman at UT around the time Tessa was flunking out. It's a huge campus, but I wonder if someone mentioned how much she favored Tessa." She paused. "But maybe Sandy Lynn already knew Wade was her father and Tessa, her half-sister."

"Maybe," Rafe conceded. "Though Jericho looked specifically for any mentions on social media posts about her father, and there weren't any. Still, her mother could have told her and asked her not to mention it."

Bree considered that, too. Wade was rich and powerful, and Nancy possibly didn't want to rock the boat with him. Or maybe she had done some boat rocking, and Wade had shut it down.

If so, that went back to Wade having lied.

Because even if he hadn't believed Sandy Lynn was his child, he should have at least mentioned there was a possibility he'd had a second daughter. Wade had been a loving, indulgent father to Tessa, but Bree knew he could also be a hard-assed businessman. If Nancy had crossed him in some way, then maybe he'd cut both her and the daughter out of his life.

"That's about it for now on Nancy and Sandy Lynn," Rafe concluded. "But Wade might be able to fill us in."

Yes, and Bree was about to drive to the gate when her phone rang, and she saw Davy's name on the dash. She silently cursed and hoped there hadn't been another emergency that required the fire chief.

"You're on speaker," she told Davy when she answered. "Rafe is listening."

"Good. Because I might have something. Remember, I told you about that party where I saw Tessa shortly before she disappeared?"

"I do," Bree confirmed. "You thought she might have been with Buckner."

"Well, she was with him, and I have proof. After we chatted, I recalled the name of the person throwing that party and went searching on her old social media pages.

Some of the photos were still there, including the one I'm sending you right now of Tessa and Buckner."

Her phone dinged, and when the photo downloaded, she saw that Davy was right. It was indeed Tessa in a strapless gold party gown. Buckner had his arm slung possessively around her bare shoulders, and he was sporting that same cocky grin.

"They both look high to me," Davy said. "Or drunk."

They did. Both Tessa and Buckner had glazed eyes, and Tessa didn't look too steady on her feet.

"I'm not sure the picture will help," Davy went on. "But it does confirm Buckner and she were once together."

"It does." Though Buckner hadn't denied knowing her. Still, this felt like more than a superficial, sex-only relationship that Buckner had made it out to be.

"Good. I hope it helps. Oh, and Rafe," Davy added. "I need to say I'm sorry again for that one off I had with Tessa. It was wrong, and it shouldn't have happened."

Rafe glanced at her, and it was a reminder of how easy it was sometimes to give into the heat. To get carried away. Oh, yes, she totally got that.

"No need to apologize," Rafe assured him. "And thanks for the photo."

Bree thanked him, too, and ended the call. Then, she focused on the task at hand. The crappy task she was dreading.

She gathered her breath again before she drove to the gate. It opened right away so maybe the housekeeper had been watching for them. But she was wrong about that. Because the moment she pulled to a stop in front of the house, Wade came out the front door.

"Loretta said you'd called and wanted to know if I was home," Wade volunteered. "What's wrong? Did you find Tessa?"

"Why don't we talk inside," Bree replied.

Of course, that put some instant fear and alarm in Wade's eyes, but she had to wonder if those emotions were for Tessa or because he knew his secret child had been uncovered?

Wade didn't take them to the living room but rather straight down the side hall to his office. Like the rest of the house, it was massive, and it had an incredible view of the pastures where some Palominos were grazing.

"Tell me," Wade insisted the moment he shut the door.

"The skeletal remains found at the inn were identified as Sandy Lynn Franklin," Bree said, and she watched his face closely for a reaction.

And she saw it.

Damn it, she saw it.

A quick intake of breath. A clenched jaw that lasted barely a blink before he sighed and dropped down into his chair.

"Franklin," he muttered. "Her mother is Nancy?"

Bree confirmed that with a nod and dragged over a chair so she could better make eye contact with him. "Tell me about Sandy Lynn and her." And then she would press him as to why he'd lied.

"Tessa's mom and I were going through a rough patch, and I had a one-night stand with Nancy after I met her in a diner where she worked. I saw her that one and only time," he insisted, looking her straight in the eyes. "And she never got in touch with me to tell me she was pregnant."

That eased some of the tightness in Bree's stomach. "Did she know your name or how to get in touch with you?"

Wade sighed, shook his head. "I didn't give her my surname. At least I don't think I did. I was dealing with a hangover and made it worse by leaving the diner with her and heading to a bar. The only reason I knew her name is I recall her making a joke, saying something like she wasn't any kin to Ben Franklin." He stopped. "She had a baby?"

"She did," Rafe said, sitting on the edge of Wade's desk.

"And you're positive she was my child?" Wade pressed.

"Yes," he confirmed. "Her DNA matched yours taken from the blood on the handkerchief."

Wade cursed. "That damn bomb," he grumbled, and for a moment Bree thought he was about to say if it hadn't been for that, then he wouldn't have known about this other daughter.

He didn't. Instead, Wade seemed to regroup.

"I had no idea my bloody handkerchief would lead to this," the man said instead.

"Obviously, neither did we. But at least now we know who she is, and we can give her mother some closure. All these years, she must have wondered what had happened to her daughter."

Wade made a noncommittal sound and dropped into a long silence. One that Rafe broke.

"Sandy Lynn was born nearly two years to the day after Tessa. And you never met her?" Rafe asked.

"No," Wade was quick to say. "Didn't even know she existed." He paused again, and he looked up at Rafe. "Why was Sandy Lynn buried here? Do you think she was killed in Canyon Ridge?"

"We don't know yet," Rafe explained. Like Bree, he had his attention pinned to Wade. "Obviously, we don't have any evidence from a crime scene, but the jacket she was wearing is being analyzed. That might give us some clues. It's possible even after all this time, there'll be some kind of trace or prints. A long shot, but possible."

"The jacket," he muttered. "The one like Tessa's."

"Yes," Bree confirmed. "But it was a larger size than Tessa's so it's definitely not hers. The lab tech thinks it might have been a fairly new jacket when it went into the grave with Sandy Lynn. So, maybe..." Now, she was the one who paused and tried to figure out the best way to say this. "Could Tessa have found out about her half-sister and had a jacket made for her?"

"No." Again, Wade's response was quick and adamant. "If Tessa had found out something like that, she would have come straight to me."

"What's your theory about the jacket then?" Rafe

asked.

"I don't know." Wade groaned and scrubbed his hand over his face. He then pulled out a bottle of Oban scotch from his desk, poured a triple shot into a cut crystal glass, and downed it. "Maybe Tessa and this Sandy Lynn crossed paths, and Sandy Lynn liked the jacket enough to have one made."

Bree couldn't dismiss that, especially since the two women were at the same university. Sandy Lynn wouldn't have actually even had to see Tessa but maybe a photo of it.

But that didn't explain how Sandy Lynn had ended up here.

"I know my dad went through Tessa's laptop after she went missing," Bree said. "And when he didn't find anything, he gave it back to you. Did you keep it? The techs are much more computer savvy now than they were eighteen years ago, and they might be able to find some deleted emails or something."

Wade was shaking his head again before she even finished. "As you know, I've kept most of Tessa's things, and I'd put her laptop back on her desk after your dad returned it. Unfortunately, the window there had a bad leak, and the laptop and desk got soaked. I had to toss them out."

That was too bad, but maybe Jericho could do for Tessa what he'd done for Sandy Lynn and access old social media stuff. Eighteen years ago, a mention of a fellow classmate named Sandy Lynn wouldn't have raised any alarms, but now it could be proof that the two had met.

And then what had happened?

Well, that was the question of the moment, and Bree could only speculate. She doubted it was a coincidence though that shortly after the second jacket had been made, Sandy Lynn had ended up dead and buried in it, and Tessa had disappeared.

"Wade, can you think of anyone who might have a deep grudge against you?" Rafe asked. "A grudge that would go back at least eighteen years?"

For a couple of moments, Wade just looked confused, and then the horror crept onto his face. "You think someone took or hurt Tessa to get back at me?"

"We have to cover all angles," Rafe said, and Bree noted Wade hadn't included Sandy Lynn in his comeback question. Perhaps because he hadn't wrapped his mind around her also being his daughter.

"Hell, Rafe. I got a lot of people pissed off at me," Wade admitted. "Nature of the beast. I'm a businessman, and sometimes, I make hard choices. You think one of those choices..." He trailed off and groaned.

"Why don't you come up with a list of people who might want to get back at you?" Bree advised. "Keep it in the timeline we're looking at. Around eighteen years ago."

He nodded, eventually. "If you think it'll help."

She wasn't sure it would, but Rafe was right. All angles had to be explored now that they knew Sandy Lynn was connected to Wade.

"What will happen?" Wade asked. "Will everyone have

to know I fathered this girl?"

Bree wished she could give him a blanket assurance this would stay secret. She couldn't. "We certainly won't be spreading it around, but news of it will get out. This is a murder investigation, and a lot of people will be coming in contact with the info. And if we catch a killer and he or she goes to trial, it'll certainly come out then."

Wade nodded and went quiet again. "I'll get to work on that list of those who might want to get back at me," he muttered. "Maybe we can talk later, after...well, after I've had some time."

Rafe and she stood, understanding that need for time. She just didn't know for certain what Wade was going to have to process.

"You believe him?" Rafe asked her the moment they were outside. She'd been about to ask him the same thing.

"I want to believe him," Bree said on a huff as they got back into the cruiser. "You?"

"Same. I want to, but Wade is a smart, resourceful man. Unless he had a lot of one-nighters, you'd think he would want to at least check the possibility he'd gotten Nancy Franklin pregnant."

"True. But maybe he just wanted to forget about it. Pretend it hadn't happened. After all, he stayed with his wife, and he likely wouldn't have wanted her to know he cheated on her."

"But?" Rafe prompted.

Bree would have definitely voiced some possible

scenarios if her phone hadn't rung. "It's dispatch," she said and answered it right away.

"Sheriff, you have a call from a Dr. Meyers. He says he wants to give you an update on his patient, Patricia McCray. Want me to put him through to you?"

"Absolutely," Bree couldn't say fast enough.

She started the cruiser so she could turn on the A/C, but she didn't drive because Bree suspected this conversation would need her full attention.

"This is Sheriff Bree O'Neal," she verified when the call came through.

"Dr. Jesse Myers," the man said. "You need to know upfront that I can't give you specific medical info on my patient. This is a skimming-the-surface update since your deputies keep calling about it."

"I understand," Bree assured him. "I'll take what you can give me." Hopefully, that would be enough to help make sense of what had happened.

"My patient is still mildly sedated and is responsive. I'll be able to start some tests soon that might give answers as to why she ended up here. According to your deputies, Mrs. McCray tried to shoot you, is that right?"

"Yes," Bree verified. "And during the gunfire, she was shouting that I killed her husband. I didn't," she added in a preemptive strike. "Her husband was found dead with a single gunshot wound to the head while I was here in Canyon Ridge. There was a suicide note, but I believe SAPD is investigating it as a suspicious death."

She hoped they were anyway. Bree was certainly suspicious, though she didn't want to get into speculation that Buckner or one of his goons had been the one to put the bullet in Gavin.

"I just got a report from SAPD about that," the doctor said. "I skimmed it, but I'll go through it in more detail in case there's something in it I can use to connect with Mrs. McCray."

"Connect?" Bree questioned.

The doctor took his time answering. "Again, skimming the surface, but I believe my patient has had some kind of break in her normal mental processing."

Bree refrained from a snarky "you think?" but that seemed obvious to her. Before Gavin's death, Patricia had seemingly been stable and raising her children. Afterward, she'd taken a gun and come after Bree.

What was key was learning what'd happened right before that.

"Judging from what I saw and heard while Mrs. McCray was shooting at me, "Bree said. "She believed I was responsible for her husband's death. She was adamant about it. Why?"

"That's the main reason I'm calling," the doctor replied. "Once the sedation began to wear off, Mrs. McCray started talking about a visitor she got. A man who knew what'd happened to her husband. And apparently, he's the one who told her you'd murdered Gavin."

"What man?" Bree demanded.

"Let me check my notes. I wrote it down because I knew you'd want to know...ah, here it is. She said the man's name is Davy Warner."

Chapter Eleven

——————— ☆ ———————

Rafe was fighting off another wave of fatigue with yet more coffee. Something he'd been doing for about nine hours now since this day had begun. This time, the double espresso had come from a drive-thru where Bree and he had made a pit stop during their marathon of errands and interviews.

A marathon that would hopefully end once they spoke to Sandy Lynn's mother, Nancy Franklin.

He doubted that would be easy. Then again, no part of this day had qualified as easy. It'd started with Buckner's visit, two chats with Wade, a phone conversation with Patricia's doctor.

And an intense in person talk with Davy.

Of course, Davy had denied going to Patricia and telling the grieving woman that Bree had murdered Gavin. It'd been the exact response Rafe had expected. Simply put, there was no motive for Davy to do something like that.

Unless Davy was a killer trying to muddy the waters and cover his tracks.

Since Rafe knew that most people were capable of doing some really bad things, and Bree had agreed, they'd decided to keep an eye out for any possible evidence that might prove Davy had indeed made that visit to Patricia. After all, Davy had known Tessa well and had admitted to having a one-off with her. If things had turned ugly between them, he could have killed her.

But that didn't explain why Tessa's half-sister was dead.

And why Dani had been murdered, too.

Yeah, there were a lot of unanswered questions about this investigation, and so far, they weren't getting the right answers. Not from Davy. Not from Dani's stepfather, Barney Salvetti, either.

They'd done the death notification, but the man had had no idea who or why someone would want to murder Dani. Then, he'd admitted he hadn't seen or heard from her in months. So, a bust.

Also, in the bust department was the chat with Honey Bear, AKA Craig Merkins, who had been decidedly more upset with news of Dani's death than her stepfather. The man had broken down into sobs.

But at the mention of "murder," Honey Bear had gone very pale and had gotten more cautious with his answers. He hadn't offered a single suggestion as to who might have killed her. So, maybe there was something, some kind of suspicion on Honey Bear's part, but the man wasn't offering up anything.

Rafe's money was still on Buckner.

The man had means and opportunity. Motive was murky though. Still, Dani had worked for Buckner for a long time so it was possible she had uncovered something about him that had gotten her killed.

Rafe looked up from the report he'd been reading on

Sandy Lynn when Bree pulled the cruiser to a stop in front of a small one-story house. It was in a modest but clean-looking neighborhood where all the houses were pretty much the same.

There was a white Ford Focus in the driveway, and according to the info Rafe had learned from the multiple calls and texts he'd made in the last couple of hours, the vehicle was registered to Nancy. It was still parked in front of the house, which meant she should be at home since this was her day off.

Bree hadn't called ahead to let the woman know they were coming because they hadn't known if Nancy might try to dodge them. After all, she would know there'd be questions about her daughter's paternity, and she might not want to answer them.

They got out, went to the door, and Bree rang the bell. They waited. Then, another ring. By the third ring, Rafe was figuring Nancy wasn't home after all, but the door finally eased open, and a woman peered out through the sliver of space of a slide lock.

"No soliciting," the woman said. Her voice was timid and cautious.

"We're not." Bree tapped her badge. "I'm Sheriff O'Neil, and this is police consultant, Rafe Cross. Are you Nancy Franklin? If so, we'd like to speak to you."

The one gray eye that Rafe could see widened, and the woman made a hoarse gasping sound. "This is about Sandy Lynn," she muttered. "You've found her. You found my daughter."

So, this was indeed Nancy, and he could hear the grief now in her voice. The dread. It'd been similar to Wade's reaction when he'd thought the bones in the grave had belonged to Tessa.

"We'd like to come in and speak to you," Bree repeated.

That didn't get Nancy moving. She stood there, the dread now an avalanche over her face. After several long moments though, she closed the door, and Rafe heard the rattle of the chain to let him know she was disengaging the lock. She then opened the door, stepping back.

She looked at them with those teary, fear-filled eyes that weren't a genetic copy of her daughter. In fact, Rafe didn't see much resemblance at all. Sandy Lynn clearly took after Wade.

"Did you find her?" Nancy asked, but then she waved that off. She went into the adjacent living room, sank down onto a floral sofa, closed her eyes, and lowered her head. "Give me a second first."

They did. Rafe and Bree went into the living room as well, sitting across from her in two chairs that were the same color yellow as the flowers in the sofa pattern. They stayed there for at least a full five minutes before Nancy finally lifted her head, her gaze spearing Rafe's.

"You knew my Sandy Lynn?" she asked him.

Rafe hadn't been expecting that. "Why do you ask?"

"Uh, because I think I saw a picture of you on her computer. Something from social media, I think. You were obviously a lot younger in the photo since Sandy Lynn ran away eighteen years ago. And you were with a pretty blonde woman in the picture."

There was a lot to consider in that handful of comments. The blonde with him in the photo had to be Tessa. And if Sandy Lynn had such a picture, then she likely knew who Tessa was.

What else had she known?

Hell, what else did Nancy know?

Rafe started with something easy. "Sandy Lynn ran away?"

Nancy nodded. "When she was twenty. She had a bad breakup with her boyfriend, and I think some girls at college were being mean to her. Sandy Lynn's, well, sensitive and doesn't always hold her tongue. That sometimes causes her to clash with people." She stopped. "Just tell me if you found her."

Bree pulled in a long breath. "Miss Franklin, I'm sorry to inform you, but Sandy Lynn is dead."

Rafe steeled himself up for Nancy to fall apart. But she didn't. Her eyes did fill with tears, but she blinked them back and swallowed hard.

"Yes," Nancy finally murmured. "I knew she was. I didn't want to believe it, but I knew it." She pressed her right fist to her heart. "A mother knows."

Rafe figured that could be true, but for those who "knew," he'd seen others where it'd been the worst kind of hellish shock. He got a flash of just such a notification. Of a mother so consumed by the sudden grief that she'd been inconsolable.

That was a memory he had to quickly push aside though. He could barely deal with that when he was alone and had time to wallow in his emotions. For now, the focus had to be on Nancy and Sandy Lynn.

"How did she die? Did she suffer? Please tell me she didn't suffer," Nancy begged. "And when can I see her?"

Those were standard questions, but Rafe knew that Bree was not going to have an easy time answering them. Death was one thing. Murder was an entirely different matter.

"Cause of death appears to be a blow to the head, so I suspect it would have been fast." She didn't address the part about when Nancy could see the remains but instead moved on to the other bit of info they could give her. "We found Sandy Lynn's remains in a grave near the town of Canyon Ridge," Bree said, and she waited, maybe to see if Nancy had a reaction to that.

She did.

"Canyon Ridge?" Nancy said on a gasp. "Someone buried her there? Who did that?"

"We don't know yet, but we're investigating it," Bree assured her. She paused. "Sandy Lynn was killed from a blow to the head, and according to the expert who examined her remains, she'd been dead about eighteen years."

Nancy seemed to freeze, her face going white. She

pressed her trembling fingers to her mouth.

"Who would do that to my daughter?" Nancy asked, and her voice was all breath, no sound.

"Again, we don't know, but we'll work hard to find out," Bree answered. "Let's go back to when she ran away. Tell me about that."

Maybe Bree was trying to get Nancy to focus on something other than murder and remains, but this trip down memory lane was necessary. It could provide vital clues that could indeed help them identify her killer.

Nancy nodded. Then, nodded several more times before she started. "As I said, Sandy Lynn had had a bad break up with a young man, Parker Livingston. They hadn't dated long, but I suppose she fell in love with him. She didn't see the breakup coming, so it crushed her."

Rafe made a mental note of the boyfriend's name and wished he could run a quick search on him. Not the time for it though.

"You also mentioned about some girls being mean to her," Bree prompted. "Do you have their names?"

Nancy shook her head. "I don't think Sandy Lynn ever mentioned that, but I know she came home crying several times. She commuted to college," she added. "To save money, she lived at home."

"Her father didn't help with her college expenses?" Bree asked.

He saw the flicker of surprise in Nancy's eyes before her gaze slid away from them. "No. He's not in the picture."

Bree moved to the edge of the chair and leaned down, trying to reestablish eye contact with the woman. "Miss Franklin, Sandy Lynn's remains were identified through DNA. And we know that her father is Wade Wainwright."

No flicker of surprise this time. Nancy gave a long sigh of resignation. "Yes," she murmured. Then, her head whipped up. "Does he know?"

"Yes," Bree verified. "We informed him that she was his daughter, and he knows that she's deceased."

Nancy opened her mouth as if ready to blurt out a question, maybe to ask how he'd reacted, but she didn't end up saying anything.

"You had an affair with Wade Wainwright?" Bree pressed.

"No. Just a one-night deal," Nancy said, confirming what Wade had told them. "I knew he was married, and at the moment, that didn't matter. I can't excuse what I did. But I got Sandy Lynn, so it turned out to be a win-win for me." Her voice broke. "And now she's dead."

More of those silent tears came, and Bree waited before aiming another question at the woman. "Did you tell Mr. Wainwright you were pregnant with his child?"

"No," Nancy was quick to say. "But I thought she might tell him."

Rafe and Bree exchanged glances. "She?" Rafe repeated. "You mean Sandy Lynn?"

"No." Nancy stared at them a moment. "Wade's wife, Arlene Wainwright."

Rafe was certain he was just as surprised as Bree. Somehow though, they managed to slap on their poker faces.

"How did his wife know?" Bree asked.

"She said her husband was prone to lapses. That's what she called it. *Lapses*," Nancy muttered it as if the word were profanity. "I truly thought it was love at first sight with Wade and me. Turned out though that it was lust at first sight for him, and the next morning, he left, and I never heard from him again. Then, about three weeks later, his wife showed up."

"How did she find you?" Rafe wanted to know.

"Apparently, she'd hired a PI to keep tabs on Wade, and the PI gave her my name and the address of the apartment where I lived then. She came to my door unannounced and proceeded to demand that I never see her husband again."

Rafe had known Arlene well enough to know that fit with the woman's personality. Appearances meant a lot to her and her socialite family, so she wouldn't have wanted an ugly divorce or rumors of her husband cheating.

"Did you know you were pregnant then?" Rafe asked.

"I'd just taken the test that day so, yes, I knew. And I was already having morning sickness, and I think that's why his wife guessed I was pregnant. In the middle of her lecture about leaving her husband alone, I had to run into the bathroom and throw up. When I came out, she demanded to know if I was pregnant, and I told her I was."

Rafe tried to imagine how Arlene would have reacted

to that. Not well at all. Again, there was that whole image she wanted to maintain.

"She was furious," Nancy continued a moment later. "But it was a cold kind of fury, if you know what I mean."

Rafe did indeed, and judging from the soft sound of agreement Bree made, so did she.

"What did Mrs. Wainwright do?" Bree pressed.

"She wrote me a check for ten thousand dollars and told me if I knew what was good for me and my bastard kid, I'd never tell anyone who fathered my child. I tore up the check," Nancy explained. "But I promised her no one would ever know. I didn't want to cause that kind of trouble for Wade. And I knew I wouldn't want my baby to have a relationship with him because he or she would have to also deal with this woman."

Nancy stopped again, and her eyes widened. "Did Wade's wife kill Sandy Lynn?" she asked on a rise of breath.

"No," Bree answered. "She passed away about two months before Sandy Lynn disappeared."

The relief seemed to flood through her, but it was temporary. She was probably glad her ex-lover's wife hadn't killed her daughter. But someone had.

And this could possibly go back to the photo Nancy had mentioned earlier.

"Do you still have Sandy Lynn's computer so you can show me the picture of me she had?" Rafe asked.

Nancy shook her head. "I'm sorry. That computer quit working years ago, and I didn't think to save anything on it.

But I remember you in the photo."

"And the woman who was with me in it," he commented. He took out his phone and pulled up a picture of Tessa. "Was it this woman?"

Nancy's expression confirmed that it was a yes. "Is she Wade's daughter?"

"She is," Bree verified. "Her name is Tessa, and she went missing around the same time your daughter did."

He watched Nancy process that. Then, she gasped. "Did someone kill them to get back at Wade?"

"We're looking into that, too," Bree assured her, and she took out her own phone to show Nancy the photo of Buckner and Tessa that Davy had sent them. "Do you recognize this man?"

Nancy got up and went closer to study it. She shook her head. "I don't think so. Who is he?"

Rafe had been hoping that Nancy would instantly know who Buckner was. Better yet, maybe she could say that was Sandy Lynn's boyfriend. Buckner, going by an alias, Parker Livingston. And maybe that was exactly what had happened. Buckner could have altered his appearance.

"Did you ever meet Parker Livingston, or do you have pictures of him?" Rafe asked.

"I'm sorry, but I don't. And I never actually met him. But Sandy Lynn did show me a photo on her phone that she'd taken of them together." Shock coated the woman's face again. "You don't think he did this to Sandy Lynn."

"We don't have anything that points to that, but we'll

161

be looking into it," Bree said.

Rafe pulled up another photo, one that Jericho had sent him in one of the reports, and he showed Nancy the picture of Tessa wearing the red leather jacket. He didn't get a chance to ask her about it before Nancy spoke up.

"That's Sandy Lynn's coat," Nancy insisted. "Why is Wade's other daughter wearing it?"

"We believe both daughters had the same coat," Bree explained. "Where did Sandy Lynn get hers?"

"It was a gift from her boyfriend. From Parker. He said he'd seen a girl on campus wearing it, and he thought it'd look good on Sandy Lynn. It must have been very expensive since it was custom-made."

That, too, had been included in Jericho's report. Not the actual cost but an estimation of about five hundred dollars. So, a generous gift. And it meant at some point this Parker had crossed paths with Tessa.

Yeah, Rafe intended to take a hard look at Parker Livingston.

"Is there anyone I can call to be with you?" Bree asked Nancy.

Nancy shook her head. "I'd rather be alone."

Bree nodded and stood. "As soon as we know what happened to your daughter, we'll let you know. I promise."

Nancy stood when Rafe did. The woman glanced at both of them. "When can I get my daughter's body...her remains?" she amended. "I'll want to bury her next to my parents."

162

"I'll have to get back to you on that," Bree said. "This is an ongoing investigation, so sometimes it can take a while, weeks or longer, for the remains to be released. But I will let you know," she added, and they made their way to the door.

They said their goodbyes and the moment they were outside, Rafe heard the woman break into the sobs she'd been holding back.

Part of him wanted to go back in and try to comfort her. But he doubted he could offer anything that would help with this.

As they got into the cruiser, Bree took out her phone. "I'm texting Detective Malley to have him send out an officer later to check on her."

Good. Again, that might not actually help Nancy, but it would relieve their minds to know there was someone looking out for the woman.

Bree put her phone away, groaned, and pressed her forehead to the steering wheel. Her immediate wince let him know that she'd hurt her stitches. He took out some pain meds he'd brought with him, but she shook her head.

"I've already taken more than I should, and my head won't stop pounding," she admitted. Despite that, she started the cruiser and drove away.

"Lack of sleep, fatigue, and information overload," he muttered. He had a possible fix for that. One she wasn't going to like, but Rafe threw it out there anyway.

"We've been out doing interviews and notifications all afternoon," he started. "And it's going on six pm. Not late, but late considering the day you've already put in."

Frowning, she glanced at him.

"Added to that," he went on, "I had only one change of clothes in my go-bag, and I used it this morning at your place. You, on the other hand, probably have a fresh go-bag in the trunk of the cruiser. So, how about we go to my house? It's on this side of Canyon Ridge so it won't take us as long to get there. We can regroup, go through all our notes and reports, eat, and then you can spend the night."

Her frown deepened.

"Not for sex," Rafe made sure to add. "Well, sex is optional," he amended to keep things light.

Then, he had to go with something that wasn't anywhere in the realm of light. "Buckner knows where you live. You don't have enough to charge him and get him off the streets, but if he blew up one crime scene to either obstruct justice or try to kill you, he could try it again."

"He has that *really good* PI on retainer," she reminded him, her voice tinged with sarcasm. "If he can find my address, he can find yours."

"True." Rafe hadn't forgotten about that. "But I have the security in place to alert us if he comes onto the grounds."

She didn't nix the idea right away. But a few seconds later, she shook her head. "I have to check in with my deputies. I should at least show up at my office after being gone all this time."

"You've been texting and calling them hourly with

reports," he reminded her. "And there's nothing new you can tell them. I have the computer equipment to maybe find that something new we need to make charges stick on Buckner."

Again, she wasn't quick to dispute that or decline his offer. But like before, the headshake came. "I don't want any illegal shortcuts."

He tried not to be offended. "I don't do illegal stuff. I'm just as much true blue as you are, but instead of a badge, I work for Ruby."

Okay, so he was offended, and Bree picked up on that. "Sorry," she muttered, and she groaned. "I'm snapping because I'm in pain and tired."

"Which is even more reason to stay at my place. We can get an early start and be in the station for the changeover between the night and day shift. That way, maybe we'll have something you can brief both groups on in person."

Like the other two times, she considered it. And she didn't shake her head. "A compromise. We'll get to your place so you can get some clothes, and then we can decide what to do from there. I think I know the way. It's out on old Henderson Road, right?"

"It is," he verified. "It's a few miles just past the bridge."

She took the turn onto the Interstate. "Since we've only eaten junk and snack food most of the day, I'm hoping you have something edible in your fridge."

"I do," he assured her. "I'm out of range for deliveries

from town, so I try to stay prepared."

"For unexpected guests," she muttered.

"Mainly for me because I don't like to go hungry, but yes, for the occasional guest. Jericho sometimes shows up after he's been out on assignment and is in the area. He does *not* keep a stocked fridge, so he raids mine often."

But Rafe thought she was silently asking something else. So, he just went with it and hoped he didn't sound like a fool.

"I'm not seeing anyone," he said. "Haven't for months. There won't be any lovers, former or ex, showing up."

Bree glanced at him again, and her frown was different this time. "Why not?" she asked.

"Excuse me?" Rafe had to say.

"Why don't you have a lover? I mean, you're hot. Really hot. If you don't have someone warming your bed, then it doesn't hold out hope for the rest of us mere mortals that we'll end up with a bed warmer of our own."

She had thrown him for a proverbial loop with that one.

"Is that a, uh, compliment?" he wanted to know.

Bree huffed. "It's the pain and fatigue talking. In addition to snapping, it makes me ramble and say things I shouldn't. Forget I brought it up."

Not in a million years. In fact, Rafe was hanging onto it, making him feel a little like a teenager who'd just gotten hit on.

"Why don't you have a lover?" he countered.

Her frown returned. "Too busy. Too tired of the fix-ups people keep arranging for me. Sometimes, it's just easier to be alone."

"I understand," he said. And he did. "There are times when I'm away on assignment for weeks. Assignments that aren't technically classified, but I can't discuss them. Someone who shares your bed probably expects to share the rest of you, too."

And there he was. Treading on ground that held a whole lot of bad memories. He couldn't go there. Not even with Bree.

"Parker Livingston," he announced, taking out his phone.

He could feel her glances and knew she had noticed the abrupt change in subject. She might even know why he'd done it. Sometimes, the worst hurts weren't the stitches and the bruises.

Sometimes, it was the scar that went all the way through you.

The one that stayed with you, no matter what.

"Parker Livingston," she repeated. "Please find out he's a murderous scumbag that I can arrest. I need to put someone behind bars for killing those two women."

Rafe accessed one of the Maverick Ops' databases and immediately pulled up the basics. "There are two with that name in Texas," he muttered and glanced through the ages to choose. It wasn't a hard choice since one was thirty-six, the same age Sandy Lynn would have been, and the other was sixty-four.

"Parker Livingston..." he read and then stopped. "Hell. This looks like a shell identity. There's nothing on him in the past eighteen years. And before that, there's way too little."

"A false identity," she muttered. "But Nancy seemed sure that it wasn't Buckner."

"No, but it could have been someone on Buckner's payroll. He was rich even back then. And remember, she never actually met him." Rafe paused. "So, let's play this out. Why would Buckner have wanted to have someone romantically involved with Tessa's half-sister? A someone who bought her an expensive coat and then apparently broke her heart?"

Neither of them immediately came up with anything, and the one thought that did come to mind seemed so out there. Still, he voiced it anyway.

"Let's assume Buckner or one of his henchmen stirred up Patricia enough for her to want to kill you. Could the other henchman or Buckner have done the same to Sandy Lynn?"

Bree made a sound to indicate she was considering that. "Maybe. Especially if Tessa had dumped Buckner, and he perhaps wanted to use Sandy Lynn to get back at her in some way." She took the turn off the Interstate toward his place. "That's a lot of ifs, and it doesn't explain how Sandy Lynn ended up dead."

No, it didn't, but Rafe had a gut feeling that Buckner

had played into not only what Patricia had done but also what had happened to Sandy Lynn. And Tessa. She was somehow at the core of this.

They rode in silence, both of them mulling it over, and Rafe kept up the mulling until she made the final turn toward his house. He took out his phone, temporarily disarming the security.

"There are motion sensors on the driveway," he explained. "And the perimeter of the house and yard."

She didn't ask why he had taken such measures. Bree likely knew that in his line of work, he made enemies. It was the same for her.

"That's a lot of yard to monitor," she muttered, her gaze sweeping around the pasture where he kept a couple of Andalusian horses.

"It is. The clearing around the house is an acre," he explained. "No trees or shrubs for anyone to duck behind if they managed to dodge the security sensors." Which wasn't very likely. Rafe knew because he'd personally tested them.

"No mansion like Wade," she added as she approached the house.

"No," he agreed. It was a two-story stone Craftsman that he'd designed from the ground up, and he'd meant it to be functional, secure, and comfortable.

"Park in the garage," he instructed and used his phone to open the garage doors of the space that was almost as large as the bottom floor of the house.

"Man toys," she said, taking in the Jeep, the ATV, two

motorcycles, one street-ready and the other off-road, and even a small RV.

"Work toys," he corrected.

She glanced at him. "Yes, like the assignment Jericho mentioned."

Rafe settled for a nod though he hadn't carried any of the vehicles there. Ruby had arranged for those on-site.

Bree parked the cruiser in the bare spot usually occupied by his truck that he'd left back at her place. He immediately closed the garage doors, and they went inside through a larger than usual mudroom area where there were various boots and gear for pretty much any season or weather. He did a voice command to reset the security system.

She stopped and touched a military jacket that still had his Combat Rescue Officer badge on it. "I looked up info on your career field," she said, running her fingers over the emblem that had an angel embracing the globe with the motto "That others may live" emblazoned beneath it. "Another term for CRO is Guardian Angel. It's what some people call Maverick Ops' operatives."

"Yeah," he verified. And he had no idea why her just mentioning it brought some old emotions to the surface. He pushed those away fast and led her through to the kitchen.

As advertised, it was stocked to the hilt. Not just the huge fridge but also the pantry.

"Wow," she muttered taking it all in. "Blue. I figured

you'd go with something more basic."

The cabinets were indeed a dark blue with white marble countertops. "I went with something that wouldn't show dirt," he said.

But it was more than that. Apparently, he wasn't a basic kind of guy when it came to his home. That's why the front of his fridge was also a security monitor. As they walked through, he saw the split screen that rotated the views of all twelve of the cameras.

"There's a work area in the living room," he said, pointing to the adjoining room. "A desktop, laptop, headphones, et cetera." He then pointed to the back stairs that fed off the kitchen. "The guestroom is the first one on the right. If you decide to stay, I'll get your go-bag from the cruiser."

Bree made a sound of almost idle agreement and wandered into the living room. Rafe silently cursed when he saw her make a beeline to the large stone fireplace. And the pictures on the mantel.

Hell.

He'd forgotten all about them, and they were some photos he hadn't especially wanted her to see.

She started at one end, her gaze combing over the pictures of his graduation from high school. Bree was in that one. Tessa, too. But Bree was the focus and not just because she was in the center. It was because in the shot, Rafe was looking at her while Tessa focused solely on the camera. And it wasn't any ordinary look he was giving Bree either.

The heat was there, even then.

She swallowed hard but didn't look at him. Bree just moved on to the next photo. One of him and his classmates in uniform after surviving hell week CRO training. They were filthy, exhausted, and damn happy since the CRO training had a sixty percent washout rate.

Bree moved on, and he knew the next one was going to pique her interest. It was him with two other CROs. Not filthy and exhausted in this one but a shot taken right before a deployment. In this one, he was in the middle, and on his right was a young female lieutenant. On his left was a grinning captain.

"You were stationed with them," she said, looking back at him.

He nodded and kept it at just that. A bare confirmation. Rafe definitely wasn't planning to spill details of the scar that went all the way through him.

"Let me get us something to eat," he said, "and if you have any bandwidth left after a high-carb meal, we can do some work."

Her gaze stayed fixed to his for a moment, as if she might press him for more about that photo. But she sighed. "Sounds good. You want some help?"

"No, I got it." He needed a moment alone. Time to make sure the barrier between the present and the past was firmly in place.

Bree muttered a thanks and went to the sofa, sinking

down on it. She made a sigh of pleasure, one that helped with the barriers because it was a sound that caused him to think of sex. Then again, sex was often on his mind whenever he was around Bree.

"This sofa is really comfortable," she let him know.

It was, and it was the reason Rafe had bought it. He'd crashed on it many times when he'd come back from a hard mission and had been too tired to make it upstairs to his bedroom.

He went into the kitchen and microwaved two frozen portions of chili made at his favorite restaurant in San Antonio. He arranged some crackers, fruit, and cheese on a serving board and took out two beers. Unless Bree's taste had changed over the years, she wasn't a wine drinker.

After assembling everything on a tray, he went back into the living room. She was no longer sitting upright but was curled up and sacked out.

Rafe didn't wake her. Instead, he put the food back in the fridge and covered her with a blanket he took off the back of the sofa. He got another blanket for him, heading for the recliner across from her. The moment he settled in, he felt the sleep coming, and Rafe didn't fight it.

He fell asleep, listening to the gentle rise and fall of Bree's breathing.

Chapter Twelve

—————— ☆ ——————

Bree woke to the sounds. Frantic words squeezed together between labored breaths and someone thrashing around.

She sat up, the movement automatically waking up her phone she was still holding, and she saw it was nearly ten pm. Not late, but she'd been asleep for...well, she didn't know. She nearly made some frantic sounds of her own when she didn't immediately recognize her surroundings. It took her a moment to realize she was in Rafe's living room, on his sofa.

And the sounds were coming from Rafe.

He was in the recliner across from her, his whole body in motion. Frantic shakes of his head. His hands grabbing out into the now dark room. His feet moving in some attempt to run in whatever nightmare had him by the throat.

"Get to her now," he gutted out. "Get to her now." Then, he groaned, a hoarse sob tearing from his throat.

That got Bree on her feet, and she hurried to him. "Rafe," she said, touching his shoulder.

Big mistake.

Big.

He bolted out of the chair, aiming his body and the strength of seemingly a dozen men all at her. He tackled her, sending both of them onto the sofa. Rafe pinned her there, his muscles iron hard and his hot breath hitting against her face.

"Rafe," she tried again. "It's me. It's Bree. You're not in that dream. You're here with me in your house."

He froze, his eyes finally opening, and even though his gaze immediately connected with hers, she thought it still took him a couple of seconds to rip himself out of whatever hell he'd been in and to realize where he was. And who was with him.

"God, Bree," he said. He let go of her as if she'd scalded him and rolled off her. Off the sofa, too, and onto the floor. He landed on his back with a hard thud.

"Rafe, are you all right?" She got up, kneeling down next to him.

"Yes," he managed. "Bad dream."

"I gathered that much."

He stayed quiet but made no attempt to get up. "What did I say?" he asked, and she didn't think it was her imagination that he was dreading the answer.

"Get to her now," Bree admitted.

Rafe squeezed his eyes shut for a moment and groaned. "Yeah," and that's all he said for a long time.

He lay there with her leaning over him. Staring up at her. And there was enough illumination from the moon filtering through the windows for her to clearly see his expression. He was out of the throes of the nightmare now, but he was deciding what or what not to tell her. She gave him an out.

"You don't have to say anything," she assured him. That's why it surprised her when he did.

"The woman in the picture," he muttered. "Her name was Lieutenant Ellie Abrahamson. She was my protégée. I was her supervisor. She was twenty-three. And I failed to save her."

Oh, mercy. That instantly watered her eyes, and she felt as if a meaty fist had just clamped around her head. She could hear every bit of the pain that he carried with him every moment of every day. Even sleep didn't give him a reprieve because it came at him in nightmares.

"I picked up her battered body from the bloody sand," he added a heartbeat later. "But I was too late."

Bree pulled him to a sitting position. And then pulled him into her arms. She kissed him. Long, hard, and deep. Hoping that the mere touch of her mouth could ease some of what he was feeling.

He didn't exactly return the kiss. Rafe went stiff and eased back from her. "Thanks," he said, attempting a smile. He failed. "A pity kiss probably isn't the way to go here."

"What if it's not all pity?" she asked, and that wasn't just a mindlessly blurted question either. Bree had actually given it a couple of seconds of thought.

Rafe stared at her. And stared. She took that as a good sign.

"It's not all pity," Bree insisted, and she kissed him again.

Man, he tasted good, like Christmas, birthday cake,

and the hottest sex all rolled into one. That taste roared through her, sending jolts of heat to every part of her body.

Especially one part.

Her center was on fire, and it'd been a while, if ever, since she'd gone from two kisses to wanting full-blown sex. Of course, this was Rafe so there didn't seem to be a mild version of making out.

"Bree," he said like a warning. He eased her back again, his gaze combing over her face, especially her forehead.

Those damn stitches were really killing the mood, so Bree gave him something else to think about. She kissed him for a third time, and she made it French. A hard, hungry kiss that seemed to snap the rest of Rafe's resolve.

Good.

This wasn't the moment for resolve, pity or junk from their past. It was for now. For her playing out a sexual fantasy she'd had about him for way too long. Of course, it wasn't an elaborate fantasy. No actual frills. Just down and dirty sex that she was certain would relieve this pressure cooker heat building inside her.

She trailed her mouth and tongue down his neck and enjoyed that hitch in his breath. Not panic or a fragment of a nightmare. All need. All heat.

All Rafe.

He didn't stay idle, thank goodness. He kissed her neck as well. And touched. Oh, yeah. He touched, sliding his hand over the front of her shirt to her breasts. Then, beneath the top where his finger skimmed over her skin.

Now, she was the one to make that hitched breath, and while she hadn't thought it possible, things began to move even faster, proving to her that Rafe was very much interested in seeing this through to completion.

Bree took things into her own hands. Literally. She unzipped him, reached in and found his boxers. Then, his hard-on.

Yes, he was interested.

Anchoring him against the sofa, she climbed back onto his lap, straddling him. And the battle of the clothes began. It would have been a much easier process if they'd just stopped kissing and touching and focused on the buttons, zippers, belts, holsters, and boots.

They didn't do that.

They grappled, bumping into each other, sometimes the contact so good, so right that it nearly caused her to climax. Bree fought that off, wanting just to savor this for as long as she could. That's why the moment she was finally able to peel off his shirt, she took the time to run her hands over his bare chest.

Toned and perfect.

The man was certainly living up to her incredibly high expectations.

She kissed his chest, running her tongue over all that perfection. Trailing her mouth, down, down, down. To his stomach. Apparently, that was a good spot for him because he fisted his hands in her hair, holding on. Giving into the pleasure of it all.

He stopped her though when her mouth landed on his boxers and his erection. Probably because he didn't want this to end with a blowjob. Rafe moved her, just enough to rid her of her jeans, boots.

Then, her panties.

And before she could stop him, he played really dirty and gave her a kiss right in the center of that heat. Right on the most sensitive part of her body. She cursed him and managed to wriggle away before he could finish her off with the best-placed kiss in the history of such things.

Bree got back on his lap, ready to take him inside her. One word stopped her though.

"Condom," Rafe muttered.

She silently cursed every single word of profanity she knew. And voiced some of them, too. Rafe, however, merely reached over to his pants. The very ones she'd shimmied off him, and he fumbled through his pocket to locate his wallet.

And a condom.

Bree wanted to cheer, and she might have accomplished it, too, but Rafe was damn fast in getting that condom on. In practically the same motion, he caught onto her hips and slipped that hard-on right into her.

The world exploded in her head.

Just as the fire exploded in her body.

She didn't care a flying fig what had set this moment into motion. Nope, didn't care. Those long, clever, hard strokes took her to the only place she wanted to go.

Rafe pushed her legs farther apart, buried himself to

the hilt, and then did it all over again. He wasn't gentle. Thank God. He was Rafe, and that made this perfect.

Bree arched her back, moving into the strokes. Sliding against every hard inch of him. It wouldn't last long, never could, but when she looked into his eyes, she realized she could have him all over again.

She kissed him when she felt the pleasure spike. Kissed him again when she was sure she could take no more.

Then, she took more.

Rafe slowed just enough to stretch out the moments, and then with just as much control, he finished her. The climax wracked through her. Through every part of her, and she thrust her hips forward to finish off Rafe as well.

Yeah, it was perfect, all right.

Rafe Cross had totally lived up to her expectations.

They collapsed against each other, her head landing on his shoulder, and they stayed that way while leveling their breaths and coming back down to earth. Bree wasn't sure she wanted to come back down though.

Her bruises had a different notion about that.

As the sex haze slowly slipped away, her aches and pains certainly made themselves known, and judging from the wince she felt Rafe make, he was experiencing pretty much the same. Added to that, her stomach growled.

Rafe chuckled. "We never did get around to eating." He looked at her, and she braced herself for him to say this shouldn't have happened.

He didn't.

Instead, he kissed her. It was slow, so slow, like sinking into something warm and wonderful. Not a kiss meant to reignite the flames. But it sort of did that. Yeah, this was Rafe.

After a very thorough kiss, he pulled back and smiled. Definitely no apology. "Let me make a pitstop in the bathroom, and then we can eat."

Her stomach liked that idea though it was her eyes that got a treat when she watched a naked Rafe make his way to the bathroom. A treat, followed by a glimpse of a scar that ran from the back of his shoulder nearly to his waist. It was well healed, but she had to wonder how he'd gotten it. Wondered, too, if it had something to do with the lieutenant who'd been killed.

And the reason Rafe had left the military.

No way would she ask about it, but Bree was hoping that one day he'd tell her. For that to happen though, there would have to be other naked encounters like this. Hopefully, more sex, too, when they weren't slammed with a murder investigation.

She considered just sitting there, waiting for his return. That way, she'd see more of his body. But after another growl of her stomach, Bree decided it was best to be clothed when they ate. It would be way too distracting to try to do that in the nude, and they really did need to eat.

Bree got up from the floor, cursing those bruises and the stitches that were making themselves known, and she was almost completely dressed by the time Rafe came back into the living room. She smiled because she definitely got round two of the peep show.

She went to him, kissed him. and might have started up a round two of making out, but he looked at her with eyes that had taken on a serious edge.

"I got the scar when I was trying to save Ellie," he said.

Bree nodded. But didn't speak. She hoped he knew her silence meant he didn't have to continue.

He did though.

"There was a second explosion," he added, "and both Ellie and I were hit with, well, all kinds of stuff. Nails, rocks, shrapnel, parts of a building. You name it." He paused. "Ellie regained consciousness for just a moment. A moment," he repeated in a mutter.

Bree couldn't keep her silence any longer. "You don't have to tell me."

"I feel as if I do." His gaze bore into her. "After what just happened between us, I feel as if I do."

She shook her head. "I don't want to bring all these old wounds to the surface."

Rafe attempted a smile. "That's the thing, Bree. The wounds are always on the surface." He stopped again, shrugged. "I'm learning to live with it."

Yes, she could see the fight he was having with himself about that. "You did rescue her," Bree blurted.

Rafe gave a quick shake of his head. "I didn't."

"You said she regained consciousness so that tells me she didn't die from not being rescued. She died because of

Delores Fossen

injuries from the second explosion."

He continued to stare at her, and she hoped that maybe that had gotten through. Yes, it was a sort of skewed logic, but she wanted him to start thinking beyond the belief that he'd failed. He'd succeeded, had done his job, and then Ellie had been killed in combat. Judging from the scar, Rafe had nearly been killed as well.

Rafe opened his mouth, but he didn't get a chance to say anything else because there was a series of soft but piercing beeps. Bree wasn't sure what it was, but it caused Rafe to spring into action. He grabbed his clothes, pulling them on while he hit a button on the flat-screen TV. It came to life, showing split images of the feed from the security cameras.

"Someone's here," he muttered.

That got her attention, and she immediately thought of Buckner. Had he realized she was here? It wasn't the hour for a visit, but then Buckner might not have a visit in mind. He could be coming after them to eliminate the people investigating him.

Bree put back on her holster while she watched the screen with Rafe. And she saw it.

Not a vehicle.

But a person walking toward the house.

It was a woman wearing dark clothes, and she was moving at a clipped pace. Not flat-out running but close.

Rafe zoomed in on her face, and he cursed under his breath. There was a moment. One frozen moment of shock before they both said the name of their visitor.

"Tessa."

Chapter Thirteen

———— ☆ ————

The moment Rafe muttered Tessa's name, he realized he'd been waiting for this. Waiting for her to show up. Still, it was a shock to see her in the flesh. Alive.

And running to his house.

"Jesus," Bree said, her own shock loud and clear in that single word.

"Yeah," Rafe agreed, and he had a quick debate with himself as to what to do. This was Tessa, all right.

But it didn't mean they could trust her.

In fact, the timing meant she was likely mixed up in the investigation. In the murder of those two women. Of Gavin. So, she could either be an intended victim or a killer.

"Keep your gun drawn," he instructed Bree.

No shocked reaction from her this time, and her quick nod told him they were on the same page. They had no idea what Tessa wanted, and they needed to take some precautions. This was not going to be an open-arms homecoming. Then again, that stark look on Tessa's face was an indication she wasn't expecting one.

However, she did seem to be expecting something.

Something not good.

She was firing glances all around, and when she shifted to the side, he saw the gun she had gripped in her hand. Hell. Had she come here to try to kill them? Had it come down to that? If so, Rafe only hoped he learned why after he restrained her, and they were hauling her off to jail.

They went to the door, Bree moving to the right side of it while he took the left. Rafe drew his Sig Sauer and continued to watch the monitor as Tessa got closer. There were more beeps. More alerts since she was triggering the motion detectors with every step she took.

Rafe continued to watch when she reached the porch, and he saw the hesitation when she started to press the doorbell. Tessa stopped, looking at the windows.

"Rafe?" she called out. Not a shout. More like an urgent whisper. "It's me, Tessa. Please let me in. I have to see you. Please," she repeated.

"Put down your gun," he responded, and again, watched to see what she'd do.

The door was bulletproof, but if she fired at it, that would tell him what he needed to know.

That Tessa had come there to kill him.

Tessa didn't fire though. She stooped, laying her gun on the porch. "I can't stay out here long. It's not safe."

Rafe wanted an explanation about that, but for now, he motioned for Bree to step back a little. She did. And he did the voice command to disarm the front door security so he could reach over and open it without setting off the alarm.

And there was Tessa.

Of course, she had aged. It'd been eighteen years, and she was no longer that fresh-faced teenager or college student. Nor was she a blonde any longer. Her long hair was now dark brown, and there was a wariness in her eyes that he'd never seen before.

There was a moment, just a flash of the memories of the past. They came flying at Rafe. Probably at Bree and Tessa, too. Tessa glanced at their guns that were now aimed at her, but if that concerned her, she didn't show it. Just the opposite. The concern showed in another of those sweeping glances she made behind her.

"It's not safe," she repeated, stepping in and closing the door. "I'm sorry for bringing this to your home, but I didn't have a choice."

"Bringing what to my home?" he demanded. Their shared past had allowed her entrance, but Rafe still wasn't ready to lower his gun. Neither did Bree.

"So very many things, but Callum Buckner is at the top of the list," Tessa said. Her voice broke, and she blinked back tears. "We need to talk. There are some things I need to tell you both. Just how secure is this place?" she tacked onto that. "Does it live up to the reputation of a Maverick Ops' guardian angel?"

"It does," Rafe verified, and without taking his attention off Tessa, he used the voice command to reactivate the security on the door. "DEFCON 2," he instructed.

Tessa shook her head. "What does that mean?"

"Defense Readiness Condition," he supplied. "Heightened alert. The security will...respond accordingly," he settled for saying, not wanting to get into the specifics.

But more cameras and sensor detectors had just been activated, including the house itself. If anyone managed to get past those cameras and detectors, the house would alert them.

"I'm going to search you," Bree insisted, and she holstered her gun while she went to pat down Tessa.

Tessa actually smiled when Bree put her against the door and started the search. "Sheriff Bree O'Neil. You got that badge you always wanted. And from everything I've researched, you're very good at your job."

Bree didn't respond to the friendly tone. She just continued the search, pulling a knife from Tessa's boot.

"My backup," Tessa muttered.

"That's it," Bree relayed to Rafe. "She doesn't even have a cell phone."

"Because they can be tracked," Tessa said. "So can cars, which is why I parked a mile away and rode a bicycle here. I left it in the ditch by the road."

Those were some serious precautions for a civilian who wasn't in his line of work, but it was expected for someone on the run. Or rather someone who'd been on the run for eighteen years.

"Tell me why you're terrified of Buckner," Rafe insisted. "What happened, and where have you been all this time?"

Tessa sighed, and even though she looked in the living room, specifically at the sofa, she didn't make a move to go in there. She simply sank down onto the floor and anchored her back against the door.

"It's a long story," Tessa said. "And not a very happy one." She stopped, glancing at both of them. Easy to take them both in at the same time since Bree and he were standing side by side. Her gaze finally settled on Bree. "I'm glad you two are together. I always thought you were better suited for Rafe than I was."

Rafe figured that surprised Bree almost as much as Tessa showing up. But Rafe happened to agree with her. Of course, he hadn't seen that way back when. He was sure as hell seeing it now though.

"Obviously, I'm alive," Tessa went on when neither of them said anything. "I've been in hiding all over the country, working when I could and living off what I took from my trust fund. For the last couple of years though, I've been living in Mexico City with a wonderful man. Simon," she murmured. "And I don't want him dragged into this."

Despite everything, Rafe thought he heard the love in her voice, and he was glad she'd found that. He doubted though he'd be glad about the other things that had happened.

"Best to start at the beginning," Tessa said. "I met Callum Buckner at a party when I was twenty." She snapped her fingers. "Instant, intense lust between us. We had sex in a closet after knowing each other for less than an hour."

Again, Rafe didn't react, and he hoped that Bree understood it didn't bother him to hear about Tessa's sexual partner. By then, Tessa and he had obviously moved on with their lives.

"The intensity continued for about a month," Tessa went on. "Sex, drugs, alcohol. One party right after another." She swallowed hard. "Then, at one of those parties, I danced too long with another man, and Buckner came unglued. Lots of yelling and accusations. So, I ended things with him. I thought I'd seen the last of him. Hoped I had," she whispered. "But I know now he was obsessed with me and had no intentions of letting me go."

"What happened?" Bree asked when Tessa fell silent.

Tessa looked at her. "I can tell you, and then you'll have to arrest me. Isn't that what military people say?" She waved that off. "But in my case, it's true."

Rafe felt Bree's arm muscles tighten. "Arrest you for what?" Bree demanded.

"Murder." Tessa sighed, and that's all she said for a long time. "About a month after I broke up with Buckner, Sandy Lynn Franklin walked up to me when I was in a bar, and she got in my face, claiming that she was my sister and that she was tired of me covering it up."

"Covering it up?" Rafe repeated. "Were you?"

"No. I didn't even know about her, but I could see the resemblance, so I believed her. She kept harassing me," Tessa went on. "I didn't want to confront my dad about it. I just wanted it to stop so I called Sandy Lynn and asked her to come over to the estate so I could have it out with her. Dad wasn't home. He was away on a long business trip, and he'd given the staff time off." She paused again. "I had a gun."

"You what?" Bree blurted.

"A gun," she repeated, wincing. "I know it was stupid. I was just going to threaten her with it. But things turned...bad. The worst kind of bad."

Hell in a handbasket. Tessa was confessing to murder.

"Damn right, it was stupid." Bree groaned. "That could be construed as premeditation, Tessa." She stopped, made a visible attempt to rein in her reaction. "Keep talking. Tell me what happened."

It took Tessa a moment to gather her breath. "I answered the door, and there she was. She was wearing a red jacket identical to mine. But I'm sure you know that part," she muttered. "What you don't know is that Sandy Lynn was going to try to ruin me."

"What do you mean?" Rafe asked.

"Someone, I suspect Buckner posing as a man calling himself Parker Livingston, had, well, manipulated her mind and her feelings. He'd gotten her to fall in love with him and then told her about me. Somehow, he convinced Sandy Lynn that I was trying to kill her so I wouldn't have any competition for our daddy's money."

Rafe thought of Patricia, of the person who'd prodded her into coming after Bree. Buckner, probably.

"How did Buckner find out Sandy Lynn was Wade's daughter?" Bree wanted to know.

"I'm not sure, but Sandy Lynn and I did look alike. I'm guessing he saw her, maybe even figured out she was my half-sister and then tried to use her to get back at me. That last part isn't a theory," Tessa added. "Buckner told me that no woman walks away from him, and that he would find a way to pay me back for breaking up with him."

Rafe jumped right on that. "When did he tell you that? After you killed Sandy Lynn?"

Tessa looked at him, and a single tear slid down her cheek. She nodded. "Sandy Lynn was convinced I was trying to kill her. Buckner had put a rattlesnake in her car. He'd made her sick by poisoning something she ate. Obviously, not enough to kill her. Just enough to make her come after me."

"Why didn't Sandy Lynn go to the cops?" Bree asked.

"Because Buckner also managed to make her believe they couldn't be trusted. That your father would cover up anything I did because Wade and he were friends."

Bree huffed. "My father would have never covered up anything."

"You and I know that. Sandy Lynn didn't, and Buckner worked her up into a very agitated state. I'm guessing with drugs. She started yelling the moment she saw me. She said she was going to ruin me, that she would let everyone know I attacked her. She was wild. Out of control. She just wouldn't stop cursing me, and when she spit in my face, I took out the gun I'd put in my pocket." She paused. "And I shot her."

"You shot her?" Bree repeated.

A bullet wound hadn't shown up on any of the bones,

but it was possible the shot hadn't hit bone and that the injury they had found—the bashed in part of the skull—had come from the fall after being shot.

"There was so much blood on her shirt," Tessa murmured. More tears came.

"You didn't call an ambulance?" Rafe asked.

"I was about to, and Buckner showed up. Later, I realized that had been his plan all along, but at the time, I gave into the panic. He told me I'd be arrested for murder and that he could help." Tessa squeezed her eyes shut for a moment, obviously trying to shut out the horrible images of that night.

"What happened next?" Rafe pressed, though he thought he knew where this was going.

"Buckner had me drive his Hummer from the house, and he hotwired Sandy Lynn's car and drove behind me. We stopped at the deep part of the river, and he pushed it in. Then, when he got back into his Hummer, he had me move to the passenger's seat, and he gave me a bottle of water. Drugged, I'm sure, because I started to feel woozy. He told me he was taking me to his place and that he'd then come back and dispose of the body. He said he could clean up so that no one would even know Sandy Lynn had been there."

"And you believed him," Bree muttered.

Tessa shook her head. "No, not really, but by then, I was fading fast. When I woke up, I was in Buckner's bed, and he calmly explained he'd cleaned up my mess, that I had nothing to worry about. That no one would ever know.

Well, as long as I stayed with him, no one would."

Rafe cursed. If Tessa's account of that night was true, and he believed it was, she had made a serious mistake allowing Buckner to help her. Especially since the man had obviously set it all up.

"How long did you stay with him?" Rafe wanted to know.

"Three months, two days," Tessa replied. "I can give you the hours if you want. He kept me shut away at his gated estate. His prisoner. His trophy. His plaything. He's a very dangerous man."

Yeah, Rafe had figured that, too. "Did he kill his former employee, Dani Dawson?"

Tessa's eyes widened, and she shook her head. "I don't know. I knew Dani. I met her before that godawful night. But I didn't know she'd been murdered. Buckner's certainly capable of murder. He's capable of anything."

Rafe was certain of that. "How'd you get away from him?"

"Pure blind luck. One night he forgot to lock the door to my suite, and I sneaked out. I didn't have any money, no phone, and I didn't want to go to anyone I knew because I didn't want to be arrested for Sandy Lynn's murder."

He could see all of this playing out, and Rafe wished he'd been there to help her. He hadn't been in love with Tessa then, but she had still been his friend.

"So, I went to a library and used the computer to transfer money from my trust fund to an account that I set up online," Tessa went on. "Fewer security measures in those days. All I needed was the password for my trust fund. I used the new account to book a hotel room online, and I stayed there for a few days. Nothing fancy. A dive so that no one would question why I didn't have an ID."

She stopped again, and several seconds passed before she continued. "The clerk at the dive hotel accepted my jewelry as payment for a fake ID that would match the name on the new account. From there, I withdrew enough cash to get out of the area. I stayed on the run, always looking over my shoulder until I met Simon."

Rafe sighed because even though she had wanted to keep Simon out of this, he'd have to know. So would Wade, and that would definitely be a bittersweet reunion. He had his daughter back, but she'd likely be going to jail.

Ironic, since Sandy Lynn's death might have been ruled an accident or negligent homicide if Tessa had just called in the police.

"Tessa," Bree said. "I'm very sorry for what you've been through. For what your father has been through by not knowing what happened to you," she tacked onto that. "But you were right. I am going to arrest you."

That had barely left Bree's mouth when the attack started.

Chapter Fourteen

———— ☆ ————

The house was suddenly filled with a series of rapid beeps as if all the security features had gone off at once. Every one of those beeps felt like a shout that something was very much wrong.

But what?

Bree spun around toward the monitors, but there didn't seem to be any movement on any of them. Of course, it was pitch black outside, and the clouds had covered the moon and stars, making everything seem eerily dark.

She whirled toward another sound. The grinding of shutters being lowered over the windows. And the TV screen flashed out a warning. Two words with a red banner across the top.

Immediate threat.

Bree's heart jumped to her throat, and she looked at Rafe for an explanation, but he had already turned, heading for a closet. He yanked out two Kevlar vests.

"Put them on," he told Tessa and her, tossing them each one, and he took out a third for himself. "They have tracking devices on them if we get separated."

She definitely didn't like the sound of that and wanted to question what could happen that would cause them to be separated. However, Bree wasn't sure she wanted him spelling out worst-case scenarios right now.

196

Bree did as Rafe had said and put on the vest. So did Tessa though Bree wasn't sure how they managed it since both of them were damn shaky.

"It's Buckner," Tessa cried out. "I know it's him. He probably had someone watching the place and saw me come here."

That was indeed possible. There were plenty of woods around Rafe's property and on the road leading up to it. Buckner's henchmen could have done surveillance from there or even set up some kind of monitoring equipment, all without triggering any of the sensor detectors.

Bree figured Buckner had someone watching her place as well, and the man had probably been irked when they hadn't gone back there. With no sensors and a bare-bones security system, Buckner and his thugs could have broken in her door and been on Rafe and her before they even knew what was happening. At least here they'd had some warning though she still had no idea what they were up against.

"God, Rafe, I'm so sorry," Tessa wailed.

Rafe didn't answer her. Instead, he kept arming himself with weapons he was taking from the closet, and he handed Bree another gun as well.

"Just a precaution," Rafe said, their gazes meeting.

She saw no fear in his eyes. Just an intense determination. He'd almost certainly faced situations like this before, but this was a first for her.

He put his full attention on the monitors when there was a series of more beeps, and Bree saw four men, all dressed in combat gear and gas masks, making their way to the house. They looked like giant insects.

But that wasn't all.

There was a whirring sound, and it took her a moment to realize it was a helicopter landing in Rafe's pasture.

Again, Rafe didn't react. He waited and watched. So did Bree, and she saw Buckner climb from the helicopter. He, too, was wearing combat clothes, and he made a show of lifting his phone. Seconds later, Rafe's own phone rang. He answered it and put it on speaker, keeping his attention pinned to the screen.

"Hello, Rafe," Buckner greeted. "I understand you have a visitor. Someone I very much want to see. Tessa, if you can hear this, you know we need to talk."

Tessa was frantically shaking her head. Clearly terrified. And on the verge of losing it. "He wants me dead because I can tell the cops he's an accessory after the fact to Sandy Lynn's murder."

That made sense to Bree. The penalty for accessory could end up being the same for the person who'd killed, and that would potentially put Buckner behind bars for a very long time. No wonder he wanted to keep Tessa a prisoner.

And now he wanted her dead.

Correction: he'd want all three of them—Tessa, Rafe, and her—dead so there would be no witnesses. It made Bree want to kick herself for not alerting someone that Tessa had arrived. That way, they could have had backup already in place.

But she immediately rethought that.

Any deputy on the grounds now would be facing certain danger. Above and beyond the call of anything they'd ever been trained to face.

"Rafe," Buckner went on after Tessa didn't speak. "My men have three China Lake grenade launchers aimed at your house." As if on cue, the four hired guns stopped, and three of them took aim. "I'm sure you know what China Lakes can do to a house. And, yes, even when a house is reinforced as yours is."

The adrenaline was already racing through her, but hearing that gave her another jolt. She muted his phone so she could ask Rafe a very crucial question.

"Can the grenades blow up the house?" she muttered.

"If he uses enough of them."

Bree had no doubts, none, that Buckner would use enough of them.

"Come on," Rafe added, hitching his shoulder toward that large closet where he'd pulled out the vests and guns. "I have an escape tunnel beneath the house."

That eased some of the tightness in her chest. Of course, Rafe would have a security measure like that, and it could end up saving them. Unless Buckner could manage to block it. The man had come prepared so he might have assumed there'd be an escape route.

"He'll kill us all," Tessa blurted. There was intense, raw panic in her voice. "And this is all my fault. It's me he wants, not you."

Rafe spoke a command to open another door inside the closet, one that she hadn't noticed earlier since it had no knob or hardware, and then he looked at Tessa. "We'll get out and regroup. Everything will be okay."

Tessa didn't move.

But the house seemed to do just that.

Three blasts, one right behind the other, rammed against the outside wall, shaking the floor beneath them. Shaking the very foundation. Pictures fell off the mantel and wall and crashed to the floor.

From the kitchen, there was the sound of breaking glass. At first, Bree thought that was because dishes were falling.

No.

The shutters and the windows were breaking, being ripped apart, and the smoke began to ooze through the house.

"Is that tear gas?" she asked, and yes, Bree heard the rising panic in her own voice.

"It is," Rafe confirmed, just as there were three more of those deafening blasts. "We need to move now."

The tear gas hit Bree, and her eyes suddenly felt on fire. She couldn't breathe either. And the tear gas just kept coming.

Tessa seemed frozen in place with her gaze fixed on Rafe. "I'm so sorry," she said as the smoke rushed toward her. "You deserved so much better than me."

And with that, Tessa threw open the door and ran out into the night.

Rafe cursed through his own coughing. "Use the tunnel," he told Bree. "It leads to the far back pasture. Just lie low there until I can get to you."

Bree tried to process what he was saying, but everything inside was shouting for her to get outside into the clean air so she could breathe. She tamped down that urge and attempted to focus on what Rafe had said.

Then, on what Rafe was doing.

He ran toward the front door, no doubt going after Tessa. With those armed thugs out there, he could be gunned down. They both could.

Bree ran toward the door, too.

No way would she use the safety of the tunnel when both Rafe and Tessa were in extreme danger.

She bolted out into the night, gulping in some much needed air, and she fired glances around to try to assess her situation. Tessa was running toward the pasture, toward the helicopter.

Rafe was right behind her.

Bree headed in that direction just as there was another triple explosion, and this time, the wall of the house seemed to groan before it gave way. The sound of it crashing blended with another sound. More gunfire.

No.

Not gunfire.

The launcher maybe, but this time, there wasn't a

blast. There were thuds as something hit the ground.

It didn't take Bree that long to figure out what they were because thick white smoke began to billow from them. This didn't smell the same as tear gas, and it didn't cause her eyes to burn, but it immediately engulfed her.

One second, she could see Rafe and Tessa.

The next second, she couldn't.

The smoke had swallowed them up, and the only thing she could do was try to run where she'd last seen them. No way would she let Rafe try to fight off Buckner and the four hired guns alone.

Bree didn't run, but she moved as fast as she could, mindful of where she was stepping so she didn't trip on something. She also tried to listen for those thugs if they approached her. But it was hard to hear anything though over the heartbeat slamming in her ears.

She stopped when she sensed some movement ahead of her. Impossible to tell who it was. And calling out to Rafe would only pinpoint her location to those men with the grenade launchers.

Could they see her?

Hear her?

Maybe if they were wearing some kind of equipment that allowed them to do that. In case they were, she ducked down, weaving through the side yard instead of a direct line. It was a way to avoid being shot, but it might work in a situation like this.

Ahead of her, she heard another sound, and this time

she knew what it was. *Tessa. Oh, God. Tessa.*

"No," Tessa shouted. "I won't let—"

Then, Tessa screamed. A blood-curdling cry of terror. Maybe even pain.

Bree maneuvered toward that scream, listening for anything else Tessa might say. But nothing. Bree only heard the slapping of the helicopter blades.

Had Tessa run to the chopper?

Maybe.

She must have seen on the security screens when Buckner had arrived in it. It was possible she'd gone straight to him, to hand herself over so she could try to save Rafe and Bree, her blood friends. But Bree knew that was a sacrifice that would be all for nothing because Buckner wanted all three of them.

There was another thud to her right. But this wasn't another smoke bomb. This was the sound of a fight. Fists hitting muscle and bone.

Rafe.

He was probably in a fight for his life with those hired gunmen. She wanted to believe all his training would be enough to save him, but he was seriously outnumbered. Added to that, Rafe would have basically been moving blind, just as she was. He could have walked right into an ambush.

Bree debated whether to go to him or Tessa. It was a damned if she did, damned if she didn't situation, so she tried to think of what Rafe would want, and she could practically hear him saying two words.

Save Tessa.

So, that's what Bree did. She followed the direction of Tessa's scream, the sound of it still echoing in her head. She needed to get to Tessa before Buckner killed her and then hurry back to help Rafe.

She picked up the pace, running now, and even though she could barely see her hand in front of her face, Bree thought she was heading in the right direction. If Buckner had Tessa, he was likely getting her on the helicopter. Then, he could take her heaven knew where to kill her.

If he hadn't already.

But Bree shoved that aside. Buckner would want to torment Tessa first. That was the kind of man he was. After all, he could have just started launching grenades at the house, ripping it apart and killing them all while they were inside. He hadn't. So, that meant Tessa was still alive.

Bree came out into a clearing that confused her at first before she realized the blades of the chopper had whipped back the smoke. The chopper was still on the ground. So were Tessa and Buckner. Buckner had Tessa in a chokehold, and Bree caught a glimpse of Tessa's terrified face.

Just a glimpse.

Before something shot into her.

The pain was instant, and she touched the point of impact. Not a bullet. Some kind of dart.

"A tranquilizer," she managed to say.

Before the world around her went dark, and she

collapsed on the ground.

Chapter Fifteen

———— ☆ ————

Get to her now!

Those were the words repeating in Rafe's head like gunfire. The images were repeating, too. Flashes of the nightmare when he'd failed to save his protégé. All of it was mixed together with new images.

Of Tessa.

Of Bree.

The smoke had gobbled both of them up. Him, too. And then the men had come after him. Fists flying. Fighting dirty.

Someone had punched him in the kidney. But he'd held his own and had broken enough bones to incapacitate three of them. The fourth, however, had shot him with a tranquilizer.

Yes, he remembered that.

Remembered falling, and then...nothing. Except there had been something. Tessa's scream. A gut-punching sound he'd heard way too much in the heat of a rescue. She was in trouble. Big, bad trouble. And he'd caught a glimpse of Bree running after her. Running to save her blood friend.

Bree!

Her name flashed through his head, too, and he forced open his eyes.

"You look like shit," someone snarled.

206

Rafe instantly went into fight mode. He looked up, assessing the situation as he sprang to his feet. It was still dark, but the smoke had cleared. And it wasn't one of the thugs who'd spoken.

It was Jericho.

"Your tracker alerted Ruby," Jericho said, tipping his head to the vest.

"Tracker," Rafe muttered, trying to get his mouth to work. He was hurting all over and remembered getting the crap beat out of him by three men. The men who were now gone.

"Once you have on the vest and then go still for more than fifteen minutes, Ruby gets an alert," Jericho reminded him.

Yeah, Rafe knew that. Hell, he'd been the one who'd designed the vests.

"Anyway, you didn't move, didn't respond when Ruby tried to call you, so she sent me," Jericho finished. "How bad are you hurt?" he asked, helping Rafe the rest of the way to his feet.

"Not bad," he lied.

"Yeah, right," Jericho said, clearly not buying that.

Rafe glanced around, trying to get his bearings and clear his head. "Still at my place," he mumbled. "But Bree and Tessa aren't."

"Tessa?" Jericho questioned. "Is she the one wearing the third vest?"

That caused a flood of information to slam through his

fuzzy brain. "Yes. Bree has one on, too. I can track them," he said, already turning to run into the house. That's when he saw that an entire wall was missing. "Hell."

Jericho made a sound of agreement. "Buckner cut your power and set your generator on fire. I'm guessing it was Buckner anyway. How many assholes did he bring with him to accomplish this?"

"Four. He was in a helicopter." Rafe snapped toward the pasture. Big mistake because it caused the pain to shoot through him. "China Lake grenade launchers. Tear gas. And smoke bombs."

"Well, the man is determined. And he got what he wanted," Jericho added, his voice turning serious. "He's got Tessa and Bree. Why exactly did he take them?"

"Tessa, because she got away from him. And because he buried Sandy Lynn's body after Tessa killed her."

"Ah. Tessa can link him to the crime. But Bree? Why her?"

Rafe could come up with several reasons. None good. "She got too close to arresting him. And he took her because he could." He cursed. "I need my phone so I can track them."

Jericho pointed to the debris on the ground. Once, that had been his phone, but it'd obviously been smashed to bits.

"Then, I need a laptop," Rafe amended. "Or Ruby can—"

"I've already tracked them on my phone." Jericho

showed him.

Rafe saw the two red dots. "Where are they?" he demanded.

"About ten miles from here at an old, abandoned compound that was once used for training a gun-running militia. It was shut down about a decade ago, but the buildings are still standing, for the most part."

Jericho pulled up an aerial view of the compound. Such that it was. It was live feed, likely being supplied by one of Maverick Ops' drones. And the drone was capturing the site all right. The metal buildings—a collection of shipping containers that had been cobbled together—were now scabbed with rust, and the weeds and underbrush were four or five feet high in places.

Rafe took it all in. The grounds. The placement of the buildings. And then he tried to take in the rest of the situation.

"Buckner left me alive," Rafe said. "The fourth asshole could have just put a bullet in my head. Why didn't he?"

Jericho pulled in a long breath. "My guess is Buckner wants to dick around with you." He shifted the view of the compound to the side of one of the outer shipping containers.

And Rafe cursed.

"Come and get them, hero," had been painted on the outside. "You can save just one."

Rafe tried not to let that feel like a punch to the throat. He failed. This sonofabitch had both Bree and Tessa, and he was making a game out of their lives.

"Let's go," Rafe insisted, heading toward the house to see what equipment he could salvage.

Jericho kept moving but stepped in front of him, facing him while he walked backwards. "You know this is a trap, right? That Buckner probably wants you there so he can kill all of us in some evil shit kind of way."

"Yeah. Can't be helped," Rafe muttered.

"Good. As long as you know what you're up against. No need to grab anything. I have everything we need in my van."

Rafe saw the van then, parked in his driveway, and he started toward it. He felt the pain with each step, but more than that, he felt the determination to do this. To get both women back. To hell with saving just one. He'd figure out a way to get them both out.

He hoped.

The doubts came though. The images of his last mission, the one where Lieutenant Ellie Abrahamson had died.

"You know, it's so much easier to remember the shitstorm missions," Jericho said as he began hauling gear from the back of his van. Earbud communicators. A replacement phone for Rafe. Guns. Knives. "They stay with you. My advice? Forget the shitstorm and focus on the guardian angel stuff. I can assist with the ass-kicking if it comes down to it."

Rafe didn't have a single doubt about Jericho's

abilities. But they were walking into a trap, and this was personal.

"You don't have to go in with me," Rafe offered.

Jericho rolled his eyes. "Shove that notion up Buckner's ass, okay?"

Rafe didn't attempt to thank the man. Nor would Jericho want it. Rafe only hoped this mission didn't get them all killed.

"Final weapon," Jericho said, pulling out a slingshot from the equipment bag, and he tucked it in one of the pockets of his camo pants.

The slingshot was famous. Or rather infamous. And Jericho always, always had it with him on missions. Maybe for sentimental reasons. Jericho had never said. But once Rafe had watched Jericho do some damage to a sniper's head, all while making no sound to alert the sniper's comrades that they were under attack.

They got in the van, and Jericho started driving while he pulled up the live feed of the compound. Rafe used his new phone to access the blueprints of the camp. When the FBI had raided it all those years ago, they'd thankfully provided a drawing of the layout in their final reports.

"Tunnels," Rafe grumbled. He tapped the spot on the dash display to show Jericho the two tunnels that fed off two of the units. "It's my guess that Buckner will have men waiting for us in those."

Jericho made a fast sound of agreement. "There are a couple of ventilation fans."

He tapped those, and they did look large enough to access the building. Still, Buckner would have made plans for that as well.

"Buckner kept me alive," Rafe said, thinking out loud. "That means he probably won't gun me down the moment he sees me. He needs something to play out."

But what?

Maybe he wanted Tessa to watch them die to make her suffer? Or was this about cleaning up loose ends and making sure no part of the murders or attacks could be linked back to him?

"What does Buckner want?" Rafe muttered. The question was meant for himself, to try to trigger his brain to come up with the right answer. The answer that would save Tessa and Bree.

"Well, either he's totally lost it and wants his revenge against Tessa served up with a dose of carnage," Jericho answered. "Or he's a calculating piece of shit with a plan to get that revenge and walk away scot-free."

"I'm going with door number two of this," Rafe said, and once again Jericho agreed.

"So, how are we getting in?" Jericho asked.

Rafe pointed to the main entrance. "I'm going in through there. You and your slingshot can go through one of the ventilation fans."

Jericho's huff let Rafe know he wasn't a fan of this, but he didn't argue. He just drove, taking turn after turn onto roads that got smaller and less traveled until they were essentially driving on a dirt and gravel trail.

When they were about a quarter of a mile away from the compound, Jericho stopped, parking the van in a cluster of trees and grabbed some more gear. Some infrared binoculars and jamming equipment to disrupt cell phone signals and cameras.

They started walking, trudging through the thick woods, which were a blessing and curse. The trees gave them plenty of cover, but there were points where they had to squeeze through the rough bark just to keep moving.

Even before the compound came into sight, Jericho activated the jamming equipment, and then they continued.

And there it was.

There was no drone in sight, but whatever Ruby had sent had done a damn good job of imaging the place. Rafe took the infrared binoculars to see what they were up against. The infrared would detect any heat sources, and they should be able to tell from the size of the sources if Tessa and Bree were here.

"One man in each of the tunnels," he relayed to Jericho. "One at each exit for a total of six."

Then, Rafe looked toward the center shipping container where he'd figured Buckner would be. And he was. Or rather a man was there whose blurry red blob matched Buckner's height and weight.

Steeling himself up, he shifted the binoculars again. Two more figures. Tessa and Bree, judging from their sizes.

They were up on some kind of platform or stage.

And then everything inside Rafe turned to ice.

Because he saw the outline of something on their torsos. Something that was generating just enough heat for the binoculars to pick it up.

"Hell," Rafe said. "Tessa and Bree have bombs strapped to them."

Chapter Sixteen

———— ☆ ————

Bree tried to blink away the wooziness. It didn't work. Everything was spinning, and her vision was too blurred to see anything.

But she could hear.

The occasional crackle of what she thought might be overhead lights. Something ticking. Footsteps. Muffled conversations.

And moans.

Someone was moaning, and Bree thought it might be someone in pain. She certainly was, but she hadn't managed to get her mouth and throat working enough to come up with any semblance of sound.

Where was she?

What had happened to her?

Again, she fought the haze that had seemingly seeped into every part of her mind. She tried some deep breaths and blinked again. Now, she could see the outline of two men, both wearing some kind of gear.

Everything came flooding back to her. And her eyes fully opened.

She'd been at Rafe's when the attack had started. An attack from Buckner and his henchmen. Tessa had run. So had Rafe and she, and they'd gotten separated. She'd heard Tessa scream and Rafe in a fierce fight with someone.

Bree wasn't exactly sure what had happened after that. The smoke had obscured pretty much everything, but she'd run toward Tessa's scream. Then, someone had shot her with a dart that was no doubt filled with some kind of sedative because she'd gone out after that.

Now, she was here.

But where was *here*?

She looked around and recognized the place from photos she'd seen. It was an old militia compound that the FBI had shut down years ago when she'd still been a deputy. There was the stench of mold and rot. Something else, too, that reminded her of a cheap plastic toy that had just been opened.

She felt the heavy weight on her chest and looked down. At first, she couldn't grasp what she was seeing. But it was there.

A bomb.

Oh, God. She was wearing a bomb.

Sticks of dynamite had been placed in the pouches of the vest that she now had on. There was a timer, too. A digital clock with a countdown on it, and it'd been turned facing her so she could see the numbers ticking off.

Twenty-nine minutes, thirteen seconds.

Her heart skipped more than a couple of beats, and her breath came out in a gust. All of it. And the muscles in her chest were vising her lungs so she couldn't drag in any air. She tried to grab the vest, frantic to get it off her, but her hands were tied behind her with what felt like rope that had been secured around a metal support pole.

"Oh, good," someone said.

Buckner.

She looked up and saw the SOB walking toward her. Bree also realized she was on some kind of elevated platform since Buckner had to go up four steps to get to her.

"You're awake." Buckner gave a cocky grin that she wished she could punch off his face. "Not her though."

Bree followed the direction of where he'd tipped his head, and her stomach dropped even more. Because Tessa was tied up against another support pole, her head slumped to the side. But she was moaning so she was alive.

They both were.

And Bree had to hold onto that. As long as they were alive, they could get out of this.

But where was Rafe?

She was too afraid to ask, but she had heard that fight. One where he'd been seriously outnumbered, so he... She stopped but couldn't hold back the hoarse sob that tore from her throat.

"Now, now," Buckner told her. "Lover boy isn't dead. My men left him very much alive, though they might have broken some bones. Maybe dislocated a few things, too." He checked the time. "They left him almost an hour ago, so I suspect he'll be here any minute now."

Bree frantically shook her head. She didn't want Rafe walking into this.

"I know, you're worried about him," Buckner went on,

the mock sympathy oozing from his voice. Behind him she saw one of his combat thugs peering out the slightly open metal door.

"What the hell do you want?" Bree demanded.

No mock tone for her. Thankfully, she'd gathered enough breath to use her cop's voice. She also began to struggle with the ropes to try to free her hands. Buckner or his thugs had obviously taken her weapons, but that didn't mean she couldn't try to fight back.

A burst of air left Buckner's mouth. Not a laugh, and the façade of any and all sympathy drained from his face. He pointed to Tessa.

"That bitch has caused me a lot of trouble. We're going to fix that tonight. Consider this a big assed tell all where I will get what I'm looking for. Or I'll kill you all," he added, and he turned and walked back toward the other man.

"Tessa?" Bree whispered, still twisting the rope. It was tight, digging into her flesh, but she kept moving her wrists. "Tessa?" she repeated.

This time, she got a reaction. Tessa opened her eyes, and Bree gave her a moment to fight off the sedatives and glance around. It wasn't a fast process. A full minute ticked off the two timers, and then Bree saw the moment it all sank in.

Tessa screamed again.

Then, she cursed, and she aimed the profanity at Buckner when she spotted him.

Buckner shifted an assault rifle he had just picked up

and came back to join them on the platform. "This stage, if you can call it that, was apparently once used for weapons' demonstrations," Buckner said as if giving them a history lesson. "And for punishment. Executions, too. From what I understand, at least a half dozen failed recruits were tied to the very poles where you both now stand, and they drew their last breaths here."

That was probably meant to scare them, but Bree wasn't scared. Not for herself anyway. She was pissed. "What do you want?" Bree repeated.

Buckner kept his narrowed eyes nailed to Tessa. "She can tell you. Can't you, Tessa? Tell them what you did after begging me to do a favor for you. After crying and pleading with me to bury your dead sister."

Tessa swallowed hard. Her eyes were hard, too, and she didn't look away from Buckner's intense stare. "I recorded the asshole saying he would help, that he would dispose of the body."

"And why did you do that, Tessa?" Buckner yelled. He took hold of Tessa's hair and slammed the back of her head against the metal pole.

Tessa gasped and cried out in pain.

"Tell her!" Buckner shouted. The man was quickly losing his grip, and that made Bree work harder to free herself. He was too far away from her to kick him, but she'd try that, too, if he got close enough.

"Because even in my state of my mind, I knew I couldn't trust you," Tessa told Buckner. "The recording was my insurance. It still is."

"Where is it?" Buckner shouted, and he reached out to ram her head into the pole again. He stopped though, and he turned away. "Soon, Tessa, I predict you'll be very eager to tell me where that recording is."

Tessa didn't get a chance to respond because the guy at the door spoke. "Boss, he's here. Just the Combat Rescue Officer."

"No," Bree muttered, and it felt as if a fist had clamped around her heart.

"You were right about him jamming our security," the thug said, glancing at a handheld monitor.

"Of course, I was right," Buckner spat out, and he hurried to join his henchman. "You're sure he's alone?"

"No one else that I can see," the man replied.

Buckner continued to watch. "Someone's probably with him. Someone staying back. Once we have him inside, keep watch."

"Rafe, no!" Bree yelled.

Buckner's gaze whipped to her, and if looks could kill, she'd be dead on the spot. But he didn't shoot her. He shifted back to where Rafe was no doubt coming closer to this nightmare.

A nightmare that would end, for her anyway, in just over twenty-four minutes, according to the timer.

But she rethought that. Would Buckner really blow them up if he didn't have the recording Tessa made? Maybe. Buckner was clearly desperate, and desperate men did dangerous things.

"Buckner?" Rafe called out.

No, no, no! Bree wanted to shout out to him again. To tell him to stay back. She had at least thought he would try to sneak up on Buckner and his hired killers.

"Well, hell," Buckner said, chuckling. "He's coming straight to the front door. The man's got balls. Watch him like a hawk," he muttered to his thug, and he opened the door even wider.

"Welcome, Rafe Cross," Buckner then shouted. "Just an FYI, if you try to gun me down, Tessa and Bree will be blown to bits. No chance of saving them." He outstretched his arms as if welcoming Rafe. "Hey, I thought you'd go all stealthy for this."

"Where are Bree and Tessa?" Rafe asked.

And then she saw him.

Wearing enough combat gear to make him look like a warrior from hell, he stepped in, glancing in Tessa's and her direction. In the same motion, Rafe took hold of the thug who'd been watching the door and punched him in the throat.

Rafe was fast. So fast. And Buckner didn't have time to react.

The guy made a strangled sound and began to fall. Rafe didn't let that happen. He dragged the man in front of him to use him as a shield.

"If you kill me, Tessa and Bree die," Buckner was quick to say. He lifted his left hand to show Rafe a device that

Bree figured would override the timers and detonate the bombs. "Of course, they could still die if time runs out. So, this is a standoff. You saw the message I painted for you outside?" He didn't wait for Rafe to answer and instead looked at Bree. "It said. *Come and get them, hero. You can save just one.*"

Sweet heaven. Buckner was torturing them. Not with physical violence. Well, other than what he'd done to Tessa. But this was mental torture, and it had to be giving Rafe the motherlode of PTSD flashbacks.

"So, to catch you up," Buckner went on, talking to Rafe now. "Eighteen years ago, the fucking bitch Tessa recorded me saying I would bury her sister's body. As you and your cop girlfriend are aware, that makes me an accessory though there are some things about that Tessa doesn't know." He waved that off. "But I'm getting ahead of myself..."

Buckner trailed off when his phone dinged, and he smiled. "Ah, the others have arrived."

Oh, no. Bree prayed they hadn't spotted someone, Jericho maybe, that Rafe had brought with him.

They waited with Rafe still holding the groaning, gasping thug. Rafe had a tight chokehold on him. Just as Buckner had a firm grip on the detonator. Bree continued to work to get the rope off her hands.

"Welcome!" Buckner called out.

And Bree stopped tugging at the ropes when the two men walked in.

What the hell were *they* doing here?

Chapter Seventeen

─────── ☆ ───────

Rafe looked at Wade and Davy as they came into the compound. He had no idea why Buckner had brought them, but he had no doubts they'd soon find out.

No doubts either that Buckner planned to kill them all.

But that was a plan Rafe had to make sure failed.

"What the hell is this?" Wade demanded. "You said you had Tessa..." He looked at the platform then, and cursing, he tried to bolt toward them.

The man who came in behind Davy and Wade put a stop to that. He muscled Wade back, pinning him to the wall. "They're both disarmed, boss. Weapons are outside."

"Tessa!" Wade shouted. There was so much emotion in his voice. Fear, confusion, anger.

Rafe was feeling plenty of those same things, and he was also battling the flashbacks from hell. He wouldn't let the past play into this though. He had to focus, had to stay ready.

All the while those numbers ticked down on the bombs.

Yeah, Rafe had seen that right away with the sweeping glance he'd first made when he'd stepped inside. He'd been right about the bombs, and unless they were just props in this dangerous game Buckner was playing, then they only had nineteen minutes and a handful of seconds. Not much time to stop what this sonofabitch had set into motion.

Another muscled man in combat clothes came in and shut the door. He gave Buckner a nod that Rafe wished he could interpret. He hoped it didn't mean Jericho had been spotted and neutralized.

Rafe glanced around. Definitely no sign of Jericho, but he saw another camo-wearing man perched up in the rafters.

"Okay, listen up, everybody," Buckner called out. "We're about to have a tell-all, and then the hero here, the former Combat Rescue Officer, will get the chance to save one of the two women. Which one will he choose? His former lover? Or his current one? We shall see."

Buckner's words were light. But not his tone or expression.

"Let's go back eighteen years when bitch Tessa recorded me saying I was going to be her accessory after the fact and bury her stupid, gullible half-sister. Yeah, I sort of tanked Sandy Lynn up on a little meth and aimed her at Tessa. Like I did to Patricia when I had her go after Tessa. But unlike the whole Tessa-Patricia deal, I didn't expect Tessa to shoot Sandy Lynn. That's not a catfight. That's murder."

Buckner stopped and looked at Tessa. "I want the recording, or your daddy dies. If that doesn't work, I kill Davy here. Poor pitiful Davy, who might be wondering why he got dragged into this shit." Buckner shrugged. "Then again, he might know exactly why."

Rafe had no idea what that meant, but damn it, Davy did look guilty of doing something. What exactly?

"Quit talking in riddles," Wade snapped. "Tell me what the fuck you want so I can get my daughter out of here."

"What I want is the recording." Buckner took on an even more lethal edge. "But unlike your love child, I am not gullible. I figure Tessa has copies stashed in multiple places, so giving me a single copy won't cut it."

Even though Tessa tried to keep a poker face, her expression confirmed that. And it made sense to have that kind of insurance against a piece of shit like Buckner.

"Once Tessa gives the locations of the recordings, I'll retrieve them," Buckner went on. "Of course, I'll have to hold her to make sure she hasn't held anything back. But all of you get to live. If you tell anyone what's happened here, then I'll make Tessa pay. Not by killing her. I was thinking of cutting off fingers, toes, ears, and, well, you get the gist." He got right in Wade's face. "Pain. Lots and lots of pain."

"You're going to pay for this," Wade snarled and looked ready to launch himself at Buckner again.

"Whoa, settle down," Buckner demanded. "And let me finish. Because step one is getting all the recordings from Tessa. Step two is a confession. Which one of you buried Sandy Lynn?" he asked, volleying his gaze between both Davy and Wade.

And there it was. The guilt practically pouring off Davy.

Hell.

"How did you get involved in this?" Rafe asked.

"What do you mean?" Tessa called out. "Buckner buried Sandy Lynn."

"Nope," Buckner said. "I'm guessing it was you." His attention settled on Davy. "It was pissing down raining when I went to get the body, just as Tessa begged me to do. But when I got there, parked on a side road and walked to the house, lo and behold I saw someone carrying poor dead Sandy Lynn in a fireman's carry over the shoulder. I couldn't tell who it was, but I snapped a couple of pictures."

Buckner pointed to one of the metal walls, and the guy in the rafter started up a projector. After a couple of moments, grainy images began to scroll across the surface. The person carrying the body was wearing a rain parka that concealed his body and face. Each step he'd taken had been captured frame by frame.

"Eighteen years ago, camera phones were a piece of shit," Buckner explained. "No way for me to tell who this was, and I didn't want to move in too close in case I got spotted. I just figured I'd let whoever it was do some dirty work for me. So, which one of you is in these pictures?" he asked Davy and Wade.

"Why does it have to be one of them?" Bree asked, still sounding like a cop despite the bomb on her chest.

The timer read thirteen minutes and eleven seconds.

Buckner sighed. "Because the man got into a silver Ford truck, and through lots and lots of research, that great private eye I have on retainer learned that only two men owned such a vehicle in your hick town." He held up his hand. "And, yes, I know you're planning to ask why I didn't just get the license plate. Well, I couldn't do that without moving out from cover because of the way it was parked."

Rafe could picture that. The rain, Buckner cowering and watching. Clicking off the pictures. But what he couldn't picture was Wade or Davy burying a body. Well, he couldn't picture it until he reminded himself that either man would likely do anything to protect Tessa.

"I managed to follow the truck to the inn," Buckner added, "but again couldn't get close enough to figure out who was playing knight in shining armor."

More blurry photos appeared on the screen. These didn't give any better angle of the truck or the man carrying the body. However, Buckner had gotten a picture of the sign that had still been in front of the inn back then.

"How did you know Tessa had killed Sandy Lynn?" Rafe asked, posing the question to both Davy and Wade.

"I didn't," Wade immediately snapped.

Davy didn't say anything. And that confirmed he was indeed the man in the rain parka. The one who'd buried Sandy Lynn.

"All right then. We're getting somewhere," Buckner declared. "I'm guessing you dropped by to see Tessa, found the body, and decided to clean up Tessa's mess." He didn't wait for Davy to confirm that. "Well, your coverup and my pictures led to another death."

"Dani Dawson's," Bree provided. "Did she see the pictures and question you about them?"

"She did more than that. She accused me of covering up a crime and said she was going to the cops. Bad idea," Buckner snarled. "Really bad."

"So, you killed her, planted her body and an explosive by the burial site," Rafe filled in. "How did you know the inn was being renovated."

"Because a friend is behind the project. Eventually, the whole place was going to be dug up, and I was...concerned. I gave Sandy Lynn that jacket that I could see she was still wearing when she was buried, and I thought maybe something on it could be traced back to me. Best to let Gavin go ahead and expose it. Then, blow it up."

"Then, you could kill Gavin and set his wife on Bree," Rafe provided.

Buckner nodded and followed it with a shrug. "Okay, since everyone is caught up, let's move to the main attraction." He lifted his hands in a grand gesture to Tessa. "Tessa will start giving me the locations of her recordings. And she'll do it now." He put a gun to Wade's head. "Daddy will be the first to die."

"There's one on a thumb drive in my purse that I left in my car on the road near Rafe's," Tessa blurted. She was crying now and shaking her head as if she couldn't believe this was happening.

Buckner smiled and nodded to the guy in the rafters, who immediately called someone. "Go on," Buckner said,

229

shifting the gun to Davy.

"The original recording is in a safe deposit box at First National Bank, downtown office, in San Antonio," she answered.

"Good girl. Continue, please." Buckner took aim at Bree, probably because he knew he wouldn't have a clean shot at Rafe.

"There's only one more, and it's on a storage cloud." Tessa stopped. "And I'll give you the password and username if you let everyone else go."

Buckner smiled. "Admirable," he chided. "But no can do."

"Tessa didn't kill Sandy Lynn," Davy spoke, and that had everyone turning toward him.

"Excuse me?" Buckner questioned.

Davy glanced at Tessa, then pinned his attention to Buckner. "She didn't kill Sandy Lynn, so you're not an accomplice after the fact. There's no reason for you to need that recording."

"What the hell do you mean she didn't kill—" But Buckner stopped. "You killed that gullible little bitch?"

Now, Davy turned back to Tessa. "I went to see you, and Sandy Lynn was coming out of the house."

"But I shot her," Tessa insisted. "I know I did."

"No," Davy muttered. He repeated it a couple of times. The pain of reliving this was in his voice, his expression. Seemingly in every part of him. "The bullet hit a thick silver locket she was wearing, and bits of the silver shattered and cut her. She was bleeding, yes, but very much alive when I saw her. And very much pissed off."

Tessa shook her head, obviously not believing this. "But she didn't move."

"Sandy Lynn told me she pretended to be dead so you wouldn't shoot her again. She said she was going to the cops to have you arrested for trying to murder her." He squeezed his eyes shut a moment. "She became hysterical, and I tried to stop her. I lost it, just lost it."

"You killed her?" Tessa asked, her voice all breath now.

Davy nodded. "Uh, I...did. I rammed her against the door and didn't stop until she...stopped."

Hell. Rafe wanted to demand why Davy had kept something like that secret all this time. It'd turned into a FUBAR with him trying to protect Tessa and then maybe trying to protect himself by burying Sandy Lynn.

"Well, what a perfect shitstorm," Buckner announced. "Why didn't you spill your guts before I confessed to a double murder?" His voice was a shout by the time he finished.

And Rafe knew what had to happen next.

Buckner had probably intended to kill, or rather try to kill, Bree, Tessa, Wade, Davy, and him. But now, there was no reason for the man to keep them alive.

Nine minutes, four seconds on the timer.

And Buckner still held the detonator that could erase even that meager amount of time. Of course, if he did let go of it, he'd be blowing up himself as well.

Rafe was ready to make his move when there was a swooshing sound followed by a grunt from the rafters. He glanced up and saw the goon there with a bloody head tumbling off the beams where he'd been perched. He spotted Jericho, too, also in the rafters on the other side. Apparently, the slingshot had come in handy after all.

The man thudded onto the floor. Not dead. But he'd likely broken something, and he staggered to get to his feet.

Then, all hell broke loose.

The thug who'd brought in Davy and Wade lifted his gun, ready to start killing. Rafe kept hold of his human shield but managed to kick the gun so the spray of gunfire went into the ceiling. Away from Tessa, Bree, and Jericho.

Rafe didn't manage to get to Buckner though before the man took aim. At Rafe. Buckner shot right through his own man, through the human shield, and if Rafe hadn't been wearing Kevlar, the shots would have almost certainly gone through him, too.

The thug that Rafe had kicked recovered and took aim at Jericho again. He fired and hopefully missed, but Rafe wasn't able to check. That's because the doors flew open, and more gunmen came flooding in. Three from the entrance. Then, three more from the side.

They all converged toward Rafe.

"Kill them!" Buckner shouted.

Rafe had no choice but to let go of the dead weight of the man that Buckner had shot. He heaved the guy right at Buckner, and Rafe dived to the side, scrambling to get behind an old oil drum.

Buckner didn't waste any time. He clicked the detonator, hopefully disarming it, and he did that so he could fire at Rafe.

Of course, the bullets blasted right through the metal of the oil drum. Rafe also heard some of the shots ricocheting, and he prayed none had hit Bree or Tessa. They couldn't get down, couldn't get out of the paths of the shots.

When Buckner had to shift his aim, Rafe shifted, too, and sent two shots right at Buckner. He was also wearing Kevlar, but one of the shots slammed into his chest, causing him to drop behind his dead comrade for cover.

Rafe made a sweeping glance around the room. Taking it all in. The seven hired guns and Buckner, all behind some form of cover. Davy and Wade on the floor behind one of the beams. Bree and Tessa struggling with their ropes to free themselves. And the timers ticking down too damn fast.

Six minutes, twelve seconds.

Rafe caught the scent of blood and had to fight the images so he wouldn't be yanked back to the desert. To the night when he'd failed. Still, some of the images got through, not enough to cause him to fail again.

He hoped.

Since he couldn't just stay put and trade shots with Buckner and the gunmen, Rafe leaned out and sent a spray of gunfire at Buckner. This time, he made sure he didn't aim for the vest. Rafe went for the upper thigh, fired, and then he immediately started moving toward Buckner.

Buckner howled out in pain and toppled over, holding onto the exact spot Rafe had intended to hit. Blood spewed from the wound, and Rafe figured the asshole had even less time left than the timers.

Just in case though Buckner wanted to try to take them all with him, Rafe snatched up the detonator and scrambled back to the side to be out of the direct line of fire from the hired guns. Since it was a simple device, he disarmed it. But stopping it didn't stop the timers. He could still see those ticking down.

"Kill them!" Buckner shouted again, but there was fear in his voice. So much fear. And if Rafe hadn't been so damn worried about getting to Bree and Tessa, he might have relished the sound of the sonofabitch dying.

The hired guns all came out from cover and lifted their weapons. Again, Rafe was the target. A big mistake because in less than a blink Jericho took out two of them. Rafe took out two as well, and the remaining pair scrambled underneath the platform and continued their attack from there, pinning down Rafe.

Four minutes, thirty-two seconds flashed on the timers.

Hell. That wasn't enough time to disarm the bombs and get everyone to safety. Still, he was going to try.

Rafe didn't have to shout out for Jericho to cover him. He would. So, Rafe bolted from cover and hoped he didn't get gunned down.

"Only time to save one," Buckner taunted. Yeah, he

was fading fast all right and was now lying in a pool of his own blood. Too weak to pick up his gun. But not too weak to add one more thing. "They'll know which one you love because that's the one you'll save."

He didn't want that to be true, and Rafe was clinging to the hope that he could save them both. He couldn't think about a choice like that. No. So, he fixed a mantra in his head.

Focus. Get to them now.

Rafe kicked Buckner's gun to the side, just in case the man managed to reach it. Wade moved in quickly to snatch it up, and he began firing at the goons. Davy grabbed one of the dead thug's guns and started to do the same.

Rafe ran as if Bree's life depended on it. Because it did.

Three minutes. Ten seconds.

Get to them now.

Rafe jumped onto the platform, heading for Bree. Just as Bree yanked herself away from the pole and threw off the ropes. She immediately started trying to unstrap the vest.

The relief nearly robbed Rafe of his breath. She had a chance.

If she would take it.

"Get the vest off and run out of the building," Rafe told her as he hurried toward Tessa. "Take Wade and Davy with you," he added, hoping that would make her obey. He wanted her as far away as possible if the damn explosives went off.

"Save yourself," Tessa muttered when he got to her.

"Don't die because of me."

"You don't have a lot of faith in my rescue skills, do you?" he said, trying to keep his voice calm while he worked furiously to get the vest off her.

Beneath the platform, Rafe heard at least one of the two gunmen yell when he was hit. There was the sound of the bullet going into flesh, followed by a thud. God knew who'd fired the killing shot, and Rafe didn't care. As far as he was concerned, this was a war zone, and he had two people to rescue while Jericho, Wade, and Davy took out the enemy.

From the corner of his eye, he saw Bree. She had the vest off and was gently laying it on the platform. Good because Rafe didn't know if was rigged to explode on contact.

"Both of you run," Tessa insisted.

They didn't. Even though it caused Rafe to curse, Bree hurried over to help him with Tessa's vest.

Two minutes flashed on the timer.

"I'm not running," Bree muttered, probably very aware that Rafe was cursing her for not saving herself.

Behind him, there was a thud, and Rafe pivoted, bracing for another attack from another would-be killer. But it was Jericho. He'd jumped down from the rafter, and he immediately took aim at something.

The final gunman who was bolting out from beneath the platform.

The gunman clearly had killing on his mind because

even though he'd already been shot, he moved his assault rifle, ready to spray everyone on the platform and go out in a hail of bullets.

That didn't happen.

Rafe whipped his own gun around, fired two kill shots into the man's head, and then immediately opened the last strap on the vest. As Bree had done with hers, he carefully lifted it off Tessa, placed in on the platform.

"Run like hell," Rafe ordered everyone.

They did. The six of them raced toward the exit, hurdling over dead bodies, weapons and the carnage caused by a blood bath.

The door seemed a million miles away, and Rafe had to slow down when Tessa tripped over a rifle. Bree slowed, too, taking one of Tessa's arms while he took the other. They raced out into the night, trying to put as much distance between them and those vests.

But the blast came too fast.

Too soon.

Roaring as if it'd come from the deepest level of hell, the explosion ripped through the night.

Rafe reached out, taking hold of Bree, pulling her to him to cover her just as she pulled him to her. They landed together, both of them shielding each other while the debris rained down around them.

Chapter Eighteen

———— ☆ ————

Bree woke with a jolt, her legs moving. Running. Her heart racing. And the images. Mercy, the images of blood and death.

So much death.

"It's all right," she heard someone say, and she snapped toward the man who'd just spoken.

Rafe.

Correction: a naked Rafe.

And he was in her bed.

One look at him—at that face!—chased away all the images. The dread. The fear. In their place came something else. Something much better.

Heat.

Pleasure.

Happiness.

It had taken a lot for them to get from point A, being slammed to the ground during the explosion on the compound to getting to point B of being naked in bed with him. In between, there'd been lots of cop chaos. Crime scene stuff. Reports. More reports. Some trips to the hospital to take care of minor injuries.

And Davy.

He'd confessed to everything he'd done to Sandy Lynn and had indeed been charged with murder and all the subsequent charges that went with concealing a crime and burying a body. Bree had had no choice but to arrest him.

And then she'd done the same to Tessa.

Bree hadn't thought in a million years she'd have to Mirandize her blood friend. But she had. And Tessa had fully cooperated. After all, she'd come back home, expecting to be arrested. The bright spot for her was she wasn't facing murder charges but some lesser ones involving obstruction of justice.

Since the initial crime had taken place eighteen years ago and wasn't murder, the statute of limitations applied. Tessa couldn't be prosecuted for her part in shooting her half-sister or failing to call for medical assistance, but she had continued to cover up the crime by storing away Buckner's confession.

Bree was hoping the charges wouldn't stick. But that was a worry for another time. She'd had to let that go when the exhaustion had claimed her body.

Then, Rafe had claimed her body as well, and he'd done a very pleasurable job of it. He'd accomplished it with some great sex that had set her up for sleep. Even if that sleep had been peppered with the dreams.

"The nightmares stay with you for a while," he said. The voice of experience.

The face of a fallen angel.

The hands of a really clever magician.

She leaned in and kissed him. Bree didn't hurry with it either. She kept it slow and ever so deep. Just enough to let him know she was glad to finally have him in her bed.

"I'm hoping this stays with me for a while, too," he said when they had to stop kissing and just breathe.

Bree shook her head. "This?"

"You. Me. Being together. You don't need me to rescue you, but..." He stopped, and she saw that he was about to make this less serious. "I have my uses," he settled for saying.

"What if I want you to rescue me?" she asked, turning the tables on him. Light but moving back to serious.

He smiled. Yeah, another weapon in his hot guy arsenal. He also kissed her and slid his hand down her breasts and to her center. Where those magic fingers began to do their thing.

Bree wanted their "thing." Or rather she wanted another round of sex with Rafe, but there was something she needed him to hear.

"Rescue me," she whispered. "By giving me something I thought I'd never have."

"What?" he asked. He continued with those maddening strokes, hitting just the right spot.

"You," Bree managed. "A chance at being with you."

He stopped, stared at her, and she was surprised that she had surprised him. But she had. She could see it in his eyes.

"You've got more than a chance of being with me. If that's what you want," he added with caution.

"It is," Bree assured him. "Because I'm thinking I care about you a lot more than I ever thought possible."

He smiled again. Definitely a weapon. But then it faded, and his eyes grew serious. "It came to me like a flash," he said. "We were running out of the compound. I reached for you, and you took my hand. That's when I knew."

"Knew what?" she murmured.

"That I love you, Bree." He kissed her then. A kiss that was as good as sex. Because this one sealed their future.

"For me, it happened when we hit the ground," she admitted. "When you pulled me into your arms. That's when I knew my life would never be the same. Because I knew then that I was in love with you."

Rafe's smile returned. "Say it again."

She did. "I love you," she managed but couldn't add more. No breath left for words.

With that smiling mouth kissing hers and his fingers at work again, Rafe sent her soaring with a climax.

———— ☆ ————

Excerpt from Lone Star Showdown

Book 2 of the Hard Justice, Texas Series

———— ☆ ————

Someone was killing him.

Jericho McKenna was well aware that was happening even though his head was pounding from the hard hit he'd taken and from the blood loss. Though it didn't take especially clear thoughts or a full 10.5 pints of blood in his body for him to figure out one thing.

He was about to die if he didn't do something now.

The trouble was—the *something* that he needed to do wasn't immediately on his mental radar. Bottom line: he was screwed six ways to Sunday.

His would-be killer had tied Jericho's hands and ankles. Had managed to disarm him, too, though that was only because Jericho had been unconscious at the time of the disarming.

So, no weapons.

No way to use his rather superb hand-to-hand combat training he'd gotten in the military. Hell, the SOB had even taken Jericho's lucky slingshot. A simple but effective little gadget that could be used to distract and rattle somebody's brain.

Or even kill.

After all, it'd worked just fine in the famous David and Goliath showdown. His would-be killer had likely realized its potential and had removed it with the other stuff. The Kevlar vest, the three knives, the Sig-Sauer and the two-inch-long Swiss mini gun that Jericho kept in his boot holster.

Along with no fighting tools, Jericho knew he had other marks against him. Massive ones. He had a deep cut on his shoulder, had been bashed on the head, popped with a stun gun and sucker punched in the kidneys. Added to that, his bindings weren't doing shit to stop him from bleeding out.

Hell in a big-assed handbasket, he didn't want to die here.

Not in this makeshift grave that the asshole killer was digging out in the middle of nowhere Texas. And he sure as hell didn't want to die until he had stopped the killer from killing again. At that moment though, he just had to figure out how to pull off a miracle.

Despite the bone-grinding agony it caused, Jericho tried to wrench the zip ties off his hands. Cops used the darn things for a reason. Because they were plenty effective in restraining bad guys.

But he wasn't a bad guy.

In fact, as an operative at Lone Star Ops, an elite security group, he often did good things, such as stopping asshole killers just like this one. And rescuing people. Saving lives. Now it was time for the lifesaver to save his own butt.

Jericho kept up the twisting and wrenching of his wrists. Kept up the thinking, too. Trying to work out anything that would help him. If he could just get a hand free, he could throat punch the killer and then make a run for it so he could regroup and ambush.

But that didn't happen.

The killer quit digging the grave and gave Jericho a fierce kick. Jericho tried to steel himself up and anchor his heels and elbows in the ground. Tried to stop himself from moving.

And he failed.

He dropped down hard into the grave, the impact causing breath-robbing pain to shoot through his body. He figured he had only seconds before the killer put an actual shot in him. A bullet that would end everything.

That didn't happen.

For a couple of seconds, the grave digging asshole stared down at him through the eye slits of the black ski mask. Then, without speaking, the killer moved.

The shovel full of dirt landed right in Jericho's face.

———— ☆ ————

About the Hard Justice Texas Series:

———— ☆ ————

The Lone Star Ops team members are former military and cops who assist law enforcement in cold cases and hot investigations where lives are on the line. Their specialty is rescuing kidnapped victims, tracking down killers and protecting those in the path of danger. Lone Star Ops is known for doing what it does best--delivering some hard justice.

About the Author:

———— ☆ ————

Former Air Force Captain Delores Fossen is a USA Today, Amazon and Publisher's Weekly bestselling author of over 150 books. She's received the Booksellers Best Award for Best Romantic Suspense and the Romantic Times Reviewers Choice Award. In addition, she's had nearly a hundred short stories and articles published in national magazines. You can contact the author through her webpage at www.deloresfossen.com.

———— ☆ ————

Hard Justice, Texas Series books by Delores Fossen:

Lone Star Rescue (book 1)
Lone Star Showdown (book 2)
Lone Star Payback (book 3)
Lone Star Protector (book 4)
Lone Star Witness (book 5)

———— ☆ ————

Visit deloresfossen.com for more titles and release dates.
Also sign up for Delores' newsletter at
https://www.deloresfossen.com/contactnewsletter.html

———— ☆ ————

Made in the USA
Middletown, DE
02 March 2024

50687663R00139